Cataclysm

Cat's Crusade
Book 3

Nik Morton

ROUGH
EDGES
PRESS

To Jennifer with love, as always for always
And of course to Hannah, Harry, Darius and Suri
And to Gordon, Maria and Tina because it's about
China
To Mark Iles, my co-conspirator for the Fighters
Magazine Taekwondo series
Thanks also to James Reasoner, Mike Bray and Jake
Bray for believing in the character, Cat

cat•a•clysm (ˈkatekliz(e)m)
n.

1. a violent geological or meteorological event
2. *fig.* a political or social upheaval

Cataclysm

Prologue

Steeped In Pain

Summer, 2018, Two weeks ago—Tenerife

As prisoner transfers went, this one was going smoothly, which was to be expected. Sergeant Inma Lopez steered her BMW R850 motorcycle ahead of the Mercedes Sprinter. She was young and keen, an exceptional officer: tall with narrow hips, an olive complexion, raven black hair tied in a bun beneath her helmet, and dark brown eyes. Bringing up the rear on his motorcycle was slightly overweight and swarthy Corporal Pepe Machado, complaining as ever about "eating dust". He grumbled a lot and had earned the sobriquet of "Moaning Machado" and yet Inma liked him: he got the work done regardless of the situation or difficulties encountered. Their small Guardia Civil procession left Playa de las Americas and steered inland onto the Arona road. This route, via Vilaflor, and through the Teide national park, may be circuitous, she allowed, but it avoided the busy main coast road, the TF-1. Once they

1

hit the TF-24, the road wended its way to El Rosario, the overcrowded prison, Penitentiary Center Santa Cruz de Tenerife II.

Handcuffed in the van, their prisoner, Alita Lopez seemed no trouble at all. Maybe she was still recovering from the trauma of the gunshot wound she'd sustained a while back. Whatever, she was now deemed fit enough to leave Hospital Sur in the center of Las Americas and go to jail to await trial.

"A simple transfer duty," Lieutenant Vargas had observed when assigning Inma and the others for this task.

Birds chirped. All was well with the world.

The curve in the road was sharp, yet easy to negotiate. But the obstruction was unexpected.

Inma braked and raised a warning gloved hand.

The Sprinter van drew to a halt behind her, its engine idling.

There'd been a small landslide. Not that uncommon.

She switched off the cycle's engine, dismounted and kicked out the stand. She raised her helmet's visor while her other hand hovered above her holster. She scanned the surrounding landscape: on the right of the road, a cluster of boulders, on the left, the fragmented slope that had caused the land-slip. No vehicles in sight, nobody about.

Breathing easy now, she sauntered toward the van, her boots crunching on small pebble debris.

Diego, the driver, opened his window, his bushy black brow wrinkled. "*Qué pasa?*"

"We need a shovel to clear this!" she called to him.

He exchanged words with his colleague riding

shotgun and then nodded and thumbed toward the van's rear. "It's in there. I'll open up."

The rear doors were unlocked and Pablo, the prisoner escort, peered out, anxiously looking left and right. "Trouble?" he asked in a high-pitched voice.

"No, just—"

A series of shots erupted from the roadside boulders. Time seemed to move slowly for Inma as she sensed the impact in her back. Disoriented, steeped in pain, she buckled on suddenly weak legs and her knees hit the hard road surface. Her vision blurred. Hazily, she watched Pablo topple from the rear of the van and hit the ground.

She saw Pepe tumble under his motorcycle, red smearing his high-viz torso; then he lay unmoving.

Glass shattered in the driver's cabin and she knew that Diego and his co-driver were slain as well.

She was having difficulty breathing, couldn't seem to move her arm, her gun useless in its holster.

Oddly, the pain had fled; now there was very little sensation at all; perhaps a last-second surge of adrenaline masked the pain.

She gulped in air but started coughing on a metallic-tasting viscous fluid.

In stark contrast to the sudden burst of deathly violence, now everything was still.

The silence persisted for a short while and then birds resumed their chirping. Inma was thankful that these would perhaps be the last beautiful innocent sounds she heard in her all too short life. Wet stickiness clung to her and a deep chilliness traced her spine.

Then she noticed a Ford Econoline van drive up and brake behind the fallen Pepe who lay motionless beneath his motorcycle. Two men got out, wearing black balaclava masks, one carrying a set of wire cutters and the other an automatic pistol. Despite being aware that her life drained from her every second, her professional mind absorbed details: they didn't wear gloves, so perhaps they didn't have criminal records. Their pace rapid, they strode to Pepe, and studied him briefly. One of them kicked him, perhaps to ensure he was dead. Her heart lurched in anguish and anger and she realized it was beating slowly, far too slowly.

A man emerged from behind the boulders, carrying an automatic rifle. He was not wearing a mask, but she didn't recognize him from any mugshots that flitted through her foggy mind. He walked toward the Sprinter's cabin and checked Diego and the co-driver and then, content that they too were dead he turned his attention to her. She wanted to close her eyes, but she couldn't. He stopped and stared at her and she waited for the coup de grace. His lips curled in the travesty of a smile. He shook his head and crossed himself, and then jogged to the Ford van. Callously, he let her live, doubtless aware that her dying moments would be filled with an overpowering rage and images of her failure.

The effects of the adrenaline had worn off, she guessed, as overpowering waves of pain racked her body and mind.

The two masked men reached the rear of the Sprinter and cautiously clambered inside. Were they here to free the prisoner or to murder her? She would never know.

Finally, all went blissfully black and the pain went away. Everything went away.

WEARING prison fatigues and handcuffed to a bracket on the interior wall of the vehicle, Alita Lopez sat on a hard bench and trembled at the sound of the gunshots. She had made plenty of enemies in her lifetime. Were they here to finish her off? Her mouth was parched as two men in balaclava masks climbed in. She held her breath and her stomach churned. She didn't want to die!

The shorter one carried an automatic pistol and warily scanned the interior. "All clear," he said over his shoulder in a nasal twang; even those two words hinted that his Spanish was a foreign tongue to him.

A tall man stepped forward, hefted a huge pair of cutters and snapped the chain of her cuffs.

She wasn't going to die! They weren't here to kill her.

Massaging her wrist still encircled with the single handcuff, she said, "Thanks, whoever you are!"

"We'll explain when we're clear of here," the short one said, helping her down to the road. He rummaged in the pockets of her dead escort officer and freed a set of keys, unlocked her cuff.

She noticed the other dead Guardia Civil officers. Blood discolored their green uniforms and yellow high-viz jackets and the road. A frisson of pleasure suffused her. All this death, solely for her benefit.

The tall man threw the cutters into the brush and all three hurried to the Ford van, which in the meantime had turned around.

They clambered into the rear and slammed the door shut.

As they motored away, the two men removed their balaclava masks.

The tall one was unfamiliar to her: lean, with Latin looks and a two-day stubble, eyes dark and brooding. The short one was clean-shaven, with a cleft chin, wide-set grayish brown eyes, high Slavic cheekbones and long tawny-brown unkempt hair dangling to his earlobes: she knew him. "Anton Belofsky!" she exclaimed. "What are you doing here?"

"Not pleased to see me, Alita?" His narrow thin lips curved.

"Of course I am. Overjoyed. But also puzzled. The last I heard, you'd run off on your boat with Jacinta Ortiz to escape the law.'

"I'm here because I have a few scores to settle."

"But why spring me free?" She raised an eyebrow, lips curling in amusement. "Not that I'm ungrateful, of course."

"I thought you'd like to get even with Whitney and Brin."

She let out a shriek. "You bet! The Whitney woman in particular! She shot me!"

"We know; we've been keeping an eye on your hospital care." He absently nibbled on a nail on his thumb. "When we heard you were fit enough to be moved to prison to await trial, it seemed the right time to act."

"I'm very glad you did."

"I'm sure that you appreciate I've taken a big risk to free you." He smiled like an alligator, mouth broad and menacing. "Perhaps you might like to return the favor?"

"Why free me to get at Whitney and Brin? Haven't you got men who would do whatever it takes for you?"

"Oh, yes, I have." He pointed at the two silent men beside them. "But I want you as my woman. You have spirit. These two targets would be my gift to you, if you are interested?"

"What about Jacinta? Wasn't she your woman?"

"We parted on amicable terms."

"I could be amicable with you, Anton. Especially after what you've done for me today."

He snickered. "Yes, I hoped you would say something like that."

"But business first," she said. "I would like to pay back the Whitney woman."

"That would please me greatly, my dear." He opened a long duffel bag and lifted out and handed her an automatic rifle.

Chapter 1

Very Bad News

Madrid

Catherine Vibrissae booked her flight to Shanghai first, using her fake Spanish passport and name, Catalina Moreno, with a return ticket scheduled for the week following her arrival. She had to book her stay in a hotel and provide an itinerary, even if she didn't stick to it; the ticket and hotel information was essential when applying for her visa from the Chinese Embassy; they were efficient, anyway: it only took a week to obtain it. She'd been careful to follow their instructions to the letter as she knew from previous visits when fashion modeling that the paperwork had to be complete and precise or annoying delays could result.

She had been quite adamant that Rick was not to join her but to stay in Tenerife under the pseudonym of Ricardo Moreno, keeping Howard Greenleaf company. To prevent him worrying, she hadn't told him about her encounter with Zabala in Tangier and on the ferry; nor had she mentioned the damage to her Toyota Land Cruiser; at least that had been repaired on the insurance; fortunately, the mechanics hadn't detected the two automatics concealed in the door panel. Rick would be pleased to know she'd now locked the guns in her Madrid apartment safe and she wouldn't be going to China with any weapons. He worried for her, and she loved him for it. No, it wasn't an easy decision for her to leave Rick behind; she missed him terribly.

And of course he was reluctant to agree, arguing on his cell-phone, "Howard's alright now. He's discovered he has a lucky streak. Most nights you'd find us at the casino in Santa Cruz. I hasten to add I don't gamble; I had my fingers burnt once, and that was enough for me. We make an odd foursome with a couple—Sara and Gene—who're working for CITES."

"Really? I wouldn't have thought there was much call for them to be working in Tenerife. There can't be much trade in endangered species on the islands, surely. Maybe Shanghai, yes, but not the Canaries."

"Apparently, Gene says, the islands serve as a conduit—a lot of cruise ships dock here, after all. He and Sara have fascinating tales to tell. I think you'd like them a lot."

"I'm sure I would." At that instant she'd envied him the lifestyle he'd recently adopted. She was tempted to cancel the Shanghai trip and join him in Tenerife. To hell with Dante, to blazes with her crusade against Ananke. Sun, shared experiences, and love-making—it was a very attractive, even a very tempting option.

"As luck would have it," Rick broke into her thoughts, "they're talking about going on to China on a case. They won't divulge anything about it, naturally."

"Lady luck has worked for us, too, hasn't it?" she whispered feelingly.

"It certainly has—we found each other—and we've got through quite a few scrapes so far. But..."

"But you don't want me to go to Shanghai, is that it?"

"Yes, damn it. This crusade of yours is getting far too dangerous."

If only he knew! She felt vindicated now that she had refrained from telling him about her fight with Zabala. "I'm sure it's probably dangerous for Sara and Gene, too. From what I've heard, trade in endangered species is big money—and the dealers are unsavory and often lethal."

"That's their job, Cathy."

"And hounding Loup Dante to the ends of the earth is *my* job. I chose it."

"Dante is unpredictable. I should know, I worked for him."

"We've been through this before, my love. I've decided. I must go and face him. End it once and for all. Then maybe I can—maybe *we* can get our lives back."

"I like that last bit. I'm not too happy about the first part, though."

"Sorry, Rick, but I've decided."

"You're so stubborn!"

"Let's not fight on the phone, Rick. Please."

He chuckled. "I'm not fighting. I'm stating a fact."

"Alright. Look, let me tell you what I've arranged. It may put your mind at ease."

Begrudgingly, he answered, "I seriously doubt it, but go ahead."

"I've phoned an old friend, Yubi."

11

"Yubi? Who's Yubi?"

"Zhu Yubi worked for Papa's firm before the takeover."

"And she lives in Shanghai, does she?"

"Close. A bit south of there, actually. A place called Jiaxing. I visited her during a fashion week I did in Shanghai a while back. She will bring round a mutual friend, too—Zheng Bingren, a journalist. Yubi's more than happy to put me up. It's a family home, a rambling old traditional building. She can provide me with details about the Ananke offices in Shanghai. From there, I can go direct and face Dante."

"Does Yubi know about this obsession of yours?"

"Of course not. Though she has no reason to like Ananke, since she was sacked shortly after the takeover, despite promises they'd keep on the original staff."

"Typical of many firms after a takeover. No honor. But why not tell her, Cathy?"

"No, I don't want her getting involved. That's why I don't want you to come with me."

"We'd become collateral damage, is that it?"

"Something akin to that, I fear. To be honest, despite the shadow of Dante falling on our reunion, it will be good to reminisce with Yubi and Zheng."

She remembered Yubi's comment: "Family home, family memories." Cat too had a surfeit of those, many of them painful now that she knew Dante was responsible for her father's death. And worse, Dante was convinced that she was actually his daughter, the consequence of an ill-judged fling he had with her mother at a bad time during her marriage. Cat shuddered at the thought.

And then a couple of days after that unsatisfactory

conversation, she got Rick's call with very bad news. News that radically altered her plans.

Tenerife

Some days before, then, predictable, like clockwork, the foursome met in the square of Santa Cruz, shook hands, exchanged kisses on cheeks and sat at one of the café's exterior tables.

Viewing through the rifle's telescopic sight, Alita recognized the tanned man with black hair—Gene Brin, damn him—and of course the blonde woman, Sara Whitney. Although they'd been present at her arrest, she hadn't a clue concerning the identities of the other two men; Belofsky hadn't bothered to get any information on them. The younger one was tall with thick black hair that also showed on his arms and the backs of his hands. He had big hands—like hams—and a big nose; the older man was tall, with a stoop, his long salt-and-pepper hair falling to his shirt collar.

Alita braced herself in the stern of Belofsky's luxury cruiser, *Benevolent Beast*, resting her elbow on the guardrail, and continued to study them.

She frowned. Sara Whitney didn't look any different, which annoyed her. The woman persisted in wearing a hat, which was *so sensible* but begged the question why did she come here if she was averse to sunshine? Whitney's sky-blue eyes were flecked with green in the shade and they complemented her long blonde hair. *Dios*, Alita remembered those damnable eyes! The woman was quite short, as she remembered,

13

and busty with a tendency to slope her shoulders. Sara Whitney curved her thin lips in a smile, displaying a wide mouth. It would be glorious to put a bullet right between those shiny white teeth, Alita mused.

She tensed. Earlier in the day, in Anton's full length cabin mirror Alita had studied her body and found its curves were not so attractive anymore; where once she'd had an hourglass figure, she'd now filled out thanks to hospital fare, and her breasts no longer resembled melons but rather partly-deflated balloons. Yet Anton found her desirable, and he'd shown that as soon as they'd been alone after her breakout. As for her caramel complexion, Alita considered it was decidedly wan. Even her hands were no longer manicured; the nails bitten back, perhaps an unwelcome trait she'd adopted from Anton.

Alita aimed at Sara Whitney's mouth, and her finger squeezed the trigger.

HOWARD GREENLEAF and Rick sat opposite Sara Whitney and Gene Brin; they all sipped café con leche, seemingly unaware of the throng of people milling about.

"I spoke to Cathy yesterday," Rick said, fidgeting nervously with the snack menu. Yet again, they had argued. "She's adamant I should stay here. Yet I find it a huge coincidence that you're both planning to go there."

Gene offered a placatory smile. "Well, we haven't got the official paperwork sorted yet. The Chinese authorities are very pernickety." His hazel eyes sparkled. "They don't want bad publicity—they've had more than enough of that!"

"I can understand their point of view," Sara said. "They've instituted bans on trading, made arrests, destroyed tons of poached ivory, but they're still stigmatized by animal activists in the west."

Rick said, "Cathy tells me there's a lot of dirty money involved—I mean, in the trade?"

Gene shifted his rugged body in his chair, stroked his cleft chin. "Yes, and there's so much money in the business that they'll kill to protect their interests. To them, human life is as cheap as the lives of the endangered species."

The waiter arrived with the clipping from the till, pinned to a plastic dish with a card.

"My turn to pay, I think," Sara said, rummaging in her capacious pocketbook.

"No, let me, I insist," said Howard, his blue-green eyes glinting. "I won again at roulette last night!" He leaned across to retrieve the dish, suddenly let out a loud grunt and slumped forward heavily onto the table. A red stain appeared on his back, spreading on his shirt, as a loud report sounded.

"Get down!" Gene barked, dragging Sara to the flagstones with him.

Rick slid off his chair and crouched awkwardly half under the table. That now familiar clinging dryness in his mouth lingered: induced by gunfire, threat, and fear.

Men and women at nearby tables shrieked and, upturning chairs, scuttled away.

Pulse racing, Rick peered over the table top and scanned the area. The shot could have come from anywhere! Was this a terrorist attack, an Islamist nutcase determined to murder tourists? Yet a single bullet—he knew all about bullets by now—didn't suggest that bleak scenario. A stray bullet, another target, perhaps?

Slowly, Gene raised his head above the level of the table cloth. "Oh, Christ!" He leaned over, his fingers touching Howard's throat. "He's still alive!" he exclaimed as the sound of sirens approached.

———

When Rick entered a room on the third floor of Nuestra Señora de Candelaria hospital, he sensed a chill run through him, but it wasn't caused by the climate control system, it was the sad sight of Howard Greenleaf lying in bed, hooked up to machines and a saline drip and God knows what else. Howard's prominent jowls were drawn, the liver spots more pronounced in his pale complexion. His salt-and-pepper hair was lank, curling to the collar of his surgical gown. Sitting at the bedside was Guardia Lieutenant Vargas, whom Rick had met earlier when giving his statement. Vargas unfolded his tall frame and they shook hands.

"How is he?" Rick asked.

The lieutenant's dark eyes reflected sadness. "He wants to speak to Mrs. Moreno."

"But ... my wife's in Madrid right now..."

"It is not for me to say, but Señor Greenleaf is anxious to speak with her before the end."

"Oh... then he knows?"

"Yes, he has been conscious on and off. The doctor told him of the prognosis."

"I can't use my phone here..." He gesticulated at the door. "I'll go and call Cathy right away."

"*Sí*. I will stay with Señor Greenleaf until you return."

NATURALLY, when Cathy learned of the shooting she expressed shock. She managed at short notice to book a flight from Madrid; it took a little over three hours. Rick's heart lifted as he easily spotted her tall physique among the crowd of tourists at Arrivals: strawberry blond to match her false passport, complexion bronzed from outdoor free rock climbing, eyes a beguiling misty blue. Heading for her thirtieth birthday in August, but she looked a decade younger. He felt guilty about being so elated to see her again. If only the circumstances had been different.

They hugged and kissed briefly in the concourse; then he hurried her outside to the hired Hyundai Santa Fe. There was no question of her going to his apartment; she insisted he drove directly to the hospital.

He led her to a waiting area quite close to Howard's room, and met Sara and Gene as well as the Guardia officer, Lieutenant Vargas.

The introductions were brief, somber. "It's good to meet you both at last," Cat said awkwardly. "Rick has mentioned you often on the phone."

Sara and Gene acknowledged this with a nod but said nothing.

"The circumstances of our meeting are tragic," Cat ended lamely.

Lieutenant Vargas cleared his throat to break the

awkwardness. "Señor Greenleaf was conscious a short while ago," he said. "He keeps phasing in and out, always asking for you, Mrs. Moreno."

"But I still cannot fathom, why him?" Cathy asked of the officer. "Do you know why he was shot?"

Vargas shrugged, absently hugging a thin black leather briefcase. "We don't know for sure, but I believe the shooter intended to kill Señora Whitney." He hunched his shoulders. "Regrettably, Señor Greenleaf got in the way."

Cathy glanced at Rick, and then at Sara.

Sara nodded, her tan seeming terribly pale at this revelation.

Rick sensed the blood drain from his own face. Had he put Howard in danger through his association with Sara and Gene? No, get the facts right, he told himself. *Howard introduced them to me, didn't he?* This was not a blame game. No, the killer was to blame, nobody else!

Cathy turned back to the lieutenant. "In that case, if you hold that theory you must have a suspicion or two?"

"I have, but no definite proof. I suspect that the shooter was a known felon, Alita Lopez."

Sara gasped. "Oh, my God! I thought she was in prison?"

The lieutenant eyed her ruefully.

"Who's this Alita Lopez?" Cathy demanded.

Her face pale, her high cheekbones flushed in contrast, Sara snapped, "A psycho." She faced Vargas. "But I don't understand. She was arrested."

"She was," Vargas replied, "but alas she was freed in a daring rescue during her transfer from the hospital to prison. Four of our officers died, one of them a female."

Gene wrapped an arm round Sara. "I'm sorry to hear that your people were killed, Lieutenant. But shouldn't you have alerted us that Lopez was at large?"

"The escape only happened a few days ago, Señor Brin. Naturally, when the bodies were discovered, the police searched the area. But Lopez and her rescuers escaped detection. Our minds were concentrated on finding them and, alas, not on informing you and Miss Whitney. We never expected either of you to be a target. We believed they had even left the island. As for Señor Greenleaf, our scene of crime officers calculate that the shot that hit him was fired from a vessel in the marina. A couple of witnesses on other boats remarked they saw what might have been the flash of a weapon discharge. One person thought he saw a woman with a rifle on a vessel, but nothing definitive. And of course several yachts had sailed by the time these witnesses came forward."

He opened his briefcase "A scrupulous search at the scene of Lopez's getaway disclosed a set of wire cutters. The owner was careless and we have identified his fingerprints; our records link him with a notorious Russian oligarch, Anton Belofsky, who has been— allegedly—involved in human trafficking. By all accounts Belofsky doesn't need the money; he does it for the kicks—and, shall we say, certain fringe benefits..."

He took out two photographs: "Anton Belofsky and Alita Lopez. Lopez's is up-to-date, Belofsky's photo is a year or so old."

Fingering the image of Alita Lopez, Sara shuddered, and then handed it to Cathy. "What shall we do?"

"After this attempt on your life, Señora, we will offer protection, naturally."

RICK PACED the hospital room while Cathy sat on the edge of the bed, her eyes tear-filled. Howard sat braced against a couple of pillows. Rick reflected that despite the life-support paraphernalia Howard didn't project the appearance of a dying man.

"As I promised, I've made all the arrangements," Howard said, his voice no longer deep and firm. "It will be completely legal."

"You're taking this very well, Howard," Rick said, stopping at the foot of the bed.

"Unlike many unfortunates that suffer sudden abrupt surcease, I am allowed to make preparations before I quit this mortal coil."

"But why me?" Cathy said, ending in a sob.

"I have no relatives. You can do something with my legacy. I want you to carry on your crusade against the big corporations that transgress like Ananke."

"Howard," Rick said, "please don't encourage her, not now, not... not..."

Cathy lanced a dark look at him.

"Not on my deathbed?" Howard gave a faint smile, eyeing Cathy. "Don't get fixated on Dante. There are plenty of others like him who need a short sharp shock."

The nurse entered and said sternly, "Please leave Señor Greenleaf now. He needs his rest."

Howard chuckled. "I'll be resting long enough soon, my dear," he told the nurse kindly.

The nurse's stony face did not register.

Winking at Cathy, Howard said, "I'll see you tomorrow."

Standing, Cathy said, "Promise?"

"I promise." His eyes glinted playfully. "We have business to transact, haven't we?"

She nodded, wiped tears from her eyes and left, her hand in Rick's.

Cathy felt warm to the touch, yet Rick feared he couldn't reach her and was incapable of consoling her.

As PROMISED, Cat and Rick appeared at Howard's bedside in the middle of the next morning. He showed them the legal paperwork and asked them to call in the doctor as a witness.

Within a minute, the papers were signed and Howard gave them to her.

Cat didn't know what to say. "Thank you" seemed inadequate. She settled for the mundane, instead: "That was quick work."

"I can still afford to pay to ensure the wheels turn swiftly," Howard said, "even in Spain. My wheels, alas, have come off completely. My journey is ended." He shut his eyes and shortly afterwards he died, still holding Cat's hand.

It was an eerie sensation, how Howard's hand slowly cooled, despite the warmth of her own clasping it tightly.

AT THE SOUTHERN INTERNATIONAL AIRPORT, the four of them watched the coffin being loaded onto the airplane, bound for London via Madrid. Howard's lawyers had arranged for him to be buried in his family plot.

Rick's spine tingled as out of the corner of his eye he noticed an officer of the Guardia Civil, his eyes vigilant, standing a short distance away.

Sara hugged Cathy. "I'm so sorry. Howard and Gerard used to tell us tales about their time with you."

That raised a smile. "I bet they did."

"Howard was a lovely man."

"Yes, he was," Cathy replied, somberly. "With a mischievous sense of humor, as you know."

Rick drove them in the Hyundai Santa Fe, discreetly tailed by a Guardia officer. Cathy sat in the passenger seat, Gene and Sara in the back. Rick glanced at Cathy. "There's no reason for me to stay in Tenerife now," he said, and added firmly, "I'll come with you to Shanghai."

She continued looking directly ahead and didn't make eye contact. "My arguments are still valid, Rick, and you know that."

He lapsed into silence for the rest of the journey.

———

CAT SENSED an awkwardness in the air as Sara and Gene whispered on the rear seat. I don't know them that well, she thought. A decent couple, but this is private, between Rick and me!

After Rick steered into the hotel approach and braked in the car lot opposite the hotel entrance, he turned to Gene. "Can I be of any assistance with your endangered species business in Shanghai?"

"I'm not sure," Gene replied cagily. "There's a lot of money involved; they're dangerous people. And to put it bluntly you're not really authorized..."

Rick wasn't going to be put off, though. "I could sniff around; see if I can learn something useful—a shipment, perhaps? Being a company lawyer might prove of some help."

"Rick," Cat said throatily, "I don't think you should."

"If you go, I go," he replied. "If you don't want me involved in your crusade against Ananke, that's fine, I can do something to help these CITES people. But I want to be near you."

Gene and Sara shifted in their seats, clearly uncomfortable about the direction of their conversation. Perhaps the mention of a crusade rang alarm bells, too.

Rick's words were hurtful, since there was no question that, if the circumstances were different and not full of potential danger, she wanted him there with her, too.

By what right did she have to dictate to him? To be fair, he was hurting as well.

He loved her and was being protective.

She should be glad about that. Shouldn't she?

Cat nodded decisively, mind made up. "Alright. You'd better fly with me to Madrid. We can also arrange your flight to Shanghai; I think there's still time to arrange a visa."

"Great!" he said, switching off the engine, beaming like a young boy granted a great favor.

Cat detected barely concealed sighs of relief from the rear seat.

———————

Madrid

After so long apart, Cat and Rick fell into each other's arms when they got inside the city apartment. No sooner had the door shut behind them, their cases shoved to one side in the hall, than they began frantically undressing each other on their way to the bedroom.

Afterwards, as they snuggled close on the bed, she said, "It still hasn't sunk in. All the money Howard has bequeathed me."

"You can do almost anything, go anywhere."

"I'm not going anywhere without you, Rick." She hugged him, kissed him on the lips.

"You don't have to continue with your crusade, you know."

"I sort of promised Howard. You were there."

"Yes, but it can be all done legally—no more abseiling down buildings!"

"We'll see—after Shanghai."

He exhaled and gave a slight nod. "Alright, I'll settle for that."

"I hope we can get the paperwork sorted and find a seat for you on the plane."

"Me too. I hated us being separated. I know it was for a good reason..." His voice choked off.

"I know, darling. I feel awful; to think we got Howard out of harm's way in Morocco only to take him to his death."

"It's sad, Cathy. But it also makes you grateful to be alive... You never know how long you've got left, do you?"

"Live for the moment?"

"Yes." He kissed her. "Something like that."

"I told you about Papa's great affection for Marcus Aurelius' *Meditations*."

"Yes, you did. So?"

"He wrote, 'In the life of a man, his time is but a moment, his being an incessant flux, his senses a dim rushlight, his body a prey of worms, his soul an unquiet eddy, his fortune dark, and his fame doubtful.' Long or short, our lives should be lived for the 'now,' not dwelled upon in the past, nor blindly yearning for an unknowable future."

"That's quite a philosophy. Seize the day?"

"I've seized something, I think..." she purred playfully.

"Hmm...so you have..."

Chapter 2

Maglev

Two weeks later—East China Sea

Perched in his leather seat high in the cockpit of the *Izolda*, his 147-foot Mangusta Oceano custom-built luxury cruiser, Anton Belofsky studied the broad muscular back of the crew-woman who steered the boat through the swell. She was competent—and diplomatic. And she needed to be, considering his companion was Alita. He turned slightly, his round hunched shoulders stretching his open-necked multi-colored shirt, while his belly overlapped garish Bermuda shorts. Next to him in the other leather chair that overlooked the control array sat Alita Lopez in a gold Dolores Cortés triangle bikini. She sipped a daiquiri while one hand idly twirled the hairs on his chest. She smelled of suntan oil and musk. Her Ray-Bans were not to protect her eyes from the sun, however, but to conceal the bruise he'd inflicted. She would have displayed it with annoying pride, he felt sure, but he requested that she be discreet, as he didn't want his two crewmen to get any silly notions about domestic violence. The bruise had nothing to do with domesticity: in a bout of anger and passion, he'd hurt her, frustrated to learn how she'd killed an innocent instead of that Whitney woman. To be fair, she'd been as disappointed.

Brin and Whitney had seriously damaged his business in Tenerife, as well as the other Canary Islands, so that he had to sell his beloved yacht *Mara* in Malta. That galled, too. Yes, it had been a risk, using Alita to get at Whitney and Brin. Even so, it sent a thrill through him to know she'd do his bidding, and even kill for him. And of course, she offered more than adequate compensation in bed.

Deeming it appropriate to flee Tenerife, they had sailed the *Benevolent Beast* to Cartagena, where it was now berthed. From there, they caught the high-speed Altaria train to Madrid and then yesterday they'd flown to Shanghai in advance of an oil symposium he was scheduled to attend. He planned to combine that with the purchase of merchandise for a select number of brothels. Alita's bruise should have receded by then, invisible with the application of a little Clinique foundation and concealer.

The triple-deck *Izolda* had been berthed in the Huangpu River, not far from the Bund, among a select handful of yachts: Sealine, Jeanneau, Sunseeker, and Princess marques, most of them. It was a good size for his purposes, with a new MTU 12v000 M53R twin diesel engine. It was fitted with all they'd require: large refrigerators, a carpeted dining room and saloon, bar and lounge, and galley finished with teak floors, the galley worktop composed of Avorite, a CD radio, Wi-Fi and LCD television with Blue-Ray DVD player. The main attraction for Alita seemed to be the Jacuzzi on the aft part of the sundeck that would accommodate five to six people. When she wasn't here in the cockpit, she lounged sunning herself on a fitted sofa there.

After a shower and a meal in their hotel, they boarded the *Izolda* and the husband and wife crew took her out to sea, pushing her to an exhilarating fifteen knots, since the swell was minimal. A couple of days away, brushed by the salt breezes, and he would feel mellow again. The angst would recede. There were still other ports of call where his female merchandise would realize a handsome profit.

His cell-phone rang and he pulled it from his shirt pocket.

It was Yegor in Tenerife. "Hello," Belofsky said gruffly. "You have news for me?"

"The body's been flown out. The woman on the hospital reception desk was helpful."

"And what did she tell you?"

"The visitors were Ricardo and Catalina Moreno. The other two you know about, Sara Whitney and Gene Brin."

"Do you know what the Morenos have to do with Whitney and Brin?"

"The nurse overheard them talking about CITES—endangered species..."

"The Morenos are involved with that organization as well?"

"I don't know, sir. It's possible."

"I think they must be CITES agents if they hang around with Whitney and Brin."

"Perhaps, sir."

"Where are they now?"

"The two couples split up. The Morenos flew to Madrid. Whitney and Brin are booked for a flight to Shanghai."

"Thank you, Yegor." He hung up.

Alita stroked his chest, and scowled. "Yegor mentioned Whitney and Brin?"

"Yes."

"I would like another chance to get rid of her, dear Anton."

He kissed her briefly on the lips. "If our path should cross with that of Whitney and Brin in Shanghai, then it will be most unfortunate for them. If not, so be it; they are of no concern to me now; they're interested only in dead animals, not live human trade."

She pouted, clearly disappointed.

"I'll make it up to you, my dear. I'm sure we can think of something to stir your blood, no?"

She curved her lips in evident anticipation.

Shanghai

The gold lucky cat stood on the windowsill, its right arm waving—a memento from Song Chong's tenure as security chief at the Nanjing plant. It had brought him much luck, he thought. Wasn't this promotion proof of that? And now he considered this was an auspicious time to trade with his visitor.

Song was aware that his appearance often intimidated people, and he was not loath to use that to his advantage. He was tall, six-four, muscular, broad-shouldered and barrel-chested. He felt out of place in a business suit sitting at a desk, but as head of Ananke security that was his lot. He wore his black hair close-cropped; however, it wasn't his bullet-head that caused concern but his sharp pointed teeth. Which could be disconcerting. He'd been told more than once that his gaze was inscrutable, and he now turned it on the man who entered his office. Mimicking the lucky cat, he waved a hand to the chair opposite and the man sat down.

Poised nervously on the edge of his chair, Jabra al-Rashid wore a smart tan suit and gripped a leather briefcase on his lap. Umber eyes stared out from a pock-marked complexion. He absently rubbed his neatly cut beard and mustache, and said in French, "When I telephoned him and explained, Monsieur Dante told me to come to see you."

"Yes," Song replied in the same language, "I have been expecting you. I trust you had a comfortable flight?" He smiled.

Jabra's eyes gave a start at sight of those teeth. He quickly collected himself, however, and said, "It was very long. I have not flown before."

"An experience, then, to be treasured?"

"Yes. It was generous of Monsieur Dante to pay my air-fare from Morocco. I hope you will be as generous when you study the documents in my possession."

"I have the authority to be generous, yes."

Jabra's nostrils flared and his tongue wetted his lips. A sign of greed if ever there was one.

"Monsieur al-Rashid, do you care to tell me what you have of such inestimable value?"

Jabra ran a hand through his kinky, black short hair

and said, "Yes." He opened the briefcase and extracted several photocopied sheets of paper. He hesitated and then slid them across the desk. "I think you are looking for these people, though you know them as Catherine Vibrissae and Rick Barnes."

The first sheet was a copy of Tangier's Continental Hotel register and showed the names Catalina and Ricardo Moreno, with their Spanish passport numbers. The second and third sheets were copies of a photocopy of the passports, in color, showing a distinct likeness of them both; hair color altered, but undoubtedly Vibrissae and Barnes. Jabra had been efficient, obtaining copies from the hotel itself. The other sheets related to the Moulay Project in the High Atlas and were of no concern to Song. Still, the information about their aliases was very useful. And a computer whizz could work on the passport photographs and produce good enlargements to be disseminated later. "This is a big help, Monsieur al-Rashid. *The journey of a thousand miles begins with but a single step.*"

"Oh, is that Confucius?"

"No, Laozi. Now, how long can you stay in Shanghai?"

"I am pleased that you are pleased, Monsieur Song. My return flight is scheduled in a week's time."

"Then you must see the sights. I will arrange for an escort. No expense spared, be assured."

"You are most generous," Jabra Al-Rashid said, bowing his head slightly.

ALTHOUGH USED TO TRAVEL, Rick found this journey the most tiring he'd ever experienced. Cathy had warned him, observing that she'd travelled to Shanghai twice for fashion weeks and a third time for a free climbing expedition in the remote Getu Valley, but that didn't make it any better for him. They boarded the Boeing 737 at Madrid's Barajas airport in mid-afternoon and took about two hours "going the wrong way," landing at Orly. They had seven hours to kill while they transferred to Charles de Gaulle, taking off in China Eastern Air's Boeing 777 not long before midnight. Sleep came easily, fortunately, and they finally arrived at Pudong airport, Shanghai late afternoon.

He felt creased and careworn, his lightweight gray suit crumpled, yet Cathy still looked cool and unfazed in her black-and white jacquard slim trouser suit.

The airport was futuristic, all glass and gleaming silver and white metal, the floors shining and spotless. He noticed an abundance of "no spitting" signs. Thankfully, direction signage was in Chinese and English, so he didn't feel completely disoriented. The personnel they encountered were polite, quiet, and appeared very efficient. He and Cathy joined the queue lined up for an unsmiling immigration officer sitting in his cubicle. Stuck in a kiosk for hours on end was no laughing matter, Rick supposed. They were waved forward individually. He observed one traveler who was having the devil of a time with his official. "They're super-efficient and miss nothing," Cathy had told him, "and are very intolerant of disorganized travelers." Fortunately, Rick had paid attention to her injunction and his documents were in perfect order.

Once they'd survived the ordeal of immigration and

retrieved their luggage, she led the way to the maglev train platform, and purchased the tickets. The low-slung slick silver train glided to the platform and the doors slid open. They stepped in and found seats.

The train accelerated for the first half of the thirty kilometer trip then decelerated during the second half; the trip lasted barely eight minutes, the train traveling at about 240kmph; an overhead text advised them of the speed: at one point it reached a maximum of 430kmph. Flat countryside sped by; they crossed many canals, and passed a good number of factories, several isolated dwellings, and dense forest, and then many building sites as Shanghai continued its expansion. Finally, they arrived at Longyang Road Station, where they transferred to the metro.

Checking the metro map, which was in English as well as Chinese, Cathy steered them to Line 2 for the northbound train. "Six stops, and then we have to change again!"

Negotiating the press of bodies and the inevitable and persistent body odor, Rick remarked, "Seems to me any time saved on the maglev is lost on switching metro lines!"

"It's still less scary than riding in a taxi, I assure you!"

They got off at Nanjing Road East, switched to Line 10, which took them under Wusong River. At the next stop they left the train and emerged into somber light of evening at Tiantong Road.

Cathy hailed a taxi.

"I thought you didn't want to risk a taxi?"

"The hotel's only a couple of minutes away. I'm not lugging the cases any further!" She checked that the cab's meter was on, and then gave directions for Broadway Mansions in faltering Mandarin. Sitting in the back, she added, "I hate the fact that we can't hire a car. It's so limiting!"

"But we passed many hire-car kiosks," Rick said, puzzled.

"Oh, we foreigners *can* opt for car rental, alright, but it comes with a driver who speaks English. Naturally, that has its advantages, but if I want to go against Ananke here, I don't want to leave an obvious trail."

"And I suppose for the same reason, taxis are out?"

"Yes, that and their cavalier attitude to other road users... I'm hoping that Yubi or Zheng will be able to drive me occasionally; for the rest, we'll have to use the trains and buses. At least I'm fairly familiar with the local transport."

"Those fashion weeks again?"

"Yes." As she predicted, only a couple of minutes passed and they turned into Suzhou Road that ran along the waterfront of Suzhou Creek. The distinctive art deco brick building dominated the roadside.

"Blimey, it's Gothamesque!" Rick exclaimed.

"It has tales to tell, I can assure you."

Opposite, on the other side of the river, stood an impressive conglomeration of skyscrapers, many of them futuristic in appearance.

Rick stepped out of the taxi cab and gasped. "What a view!"

The porter approached and took their cases while Cathy paid the taxi driver. "Wait until you go up to the restaurant, darling," she said. "The view's really spectacular at night."

Song Chong grabbed his desk phone on the second ring; the call was from his replacement in the Nanjing plant. "What is it, Heng? Do you have a problem?"

"I think so, sir. It's about Mr. Ying..."

Ying, the factory chief? Song had never liked the man. He was a time-server, now in his early fifties and aloof from his staff; more interested in his clothes than people. "What about him?"

"Before you left, sir, did you notice anything in his manner that would cause concern?"

"No, Heng, I did not. I would have briefed you otherwise. Ying and I did not get along, but he always behaved with the utmost probity as far as I was concerned."

"Oh..."

"Where are you going with this, Heng?"

"I fear that Ying is involved in something illegal..."

"In what way, illegal?"

"It is too early to say, sir. I have overheard him talking with some of the night-shift, discussing a 'special shipment'—but I don't know of anything of the kind."

"That is true, Heng. Nanjing factory has no such thing. All the shipments are the same; there's nothing special about any of them."

"That's what troubles me. What should I do, sir?"

"You're head of security now. I suggest you stay alert and try to investigate. But be careful. Oh, and I appreciate that you have brought this to my attention."

"Thank you, sir. Yes, I will do as you say." Heng closed the connection.

Heng had indeed done well, Song mused.

Why hadn't I discovered this "special shipment," whatever it is? Perhaps the arrangement only began after I left the plant?

He knew that Monsieur Dante was not averse to bending rules, but would he get involved in something illegal? Yes, of course he was capable; that business in Barcelona proved it; slick damage control ensured that it was tidied up, the blame apportioned elsewhere, but Song knew for a fact that Dante had been deeply involved. Now, was Mr. Dante aware of the "special shipment"?

There was no immediate answer to that. It might be prudent to wait, to sit on this information for a while, perhaps until Heng reported again. As Confucius opined, *The cautious seldom err.*

His phone rang.

He answered it immediately. Surely it wasn't Heng ringing back? No, the caller-ID was anonymous. "Hello?"

"Mr. Song. This is Li at Pu Dong."

"I am pleased to hear from you," Song said. "You have something to report?"

"Yes. I have instituted the new checks you gave me." Li was always the same, forthright, to the point, no finesse. Still, he was useful. "The flight manifest for China Eastern Air in from Paris lists the Moreno couple you're enquiring about. They arrived two hours ago."

Two hours! "Thank you." He could be just as abrupt; he hung up. Bad timing. *If only I'd spoken to Jabra earlier!*

Vibrissae would need a native-speaker as a contact, so whom would she meet here?

He stood and went to the filing cabinet and pulled out the document folder and checked the pages again. Two names stood out. Zhu Yubi was a friend and fellow chemist who had worked for the Vibrissae firm before Ananke took it over. The other was Zheng Bingren, a journalist working on the *Shanghai Daily*; they'd met at university, apparently.

Time to call in Deshi and Enlai, and pay a little visit.

Chapter 3

Alternative to Sleep

C at had booked an economy room, with large double beds facing a huge television in its mahogany housing.

They unpacked, showered and changed.

Later, they dined in the Belle Vue Restaurant on the second floor, their window table providing a view of Waibaidu Bridge, where the Huangpu and Suzhou rivers met. Below was the Bund, a broad promenade lined with colonial buildings and opposite, the mesmerizing modern Shanghai skyline—myriad lights, reds, greens, whites, blues, and gold. She always found the vista enchanting.

They raised and clinked their glasses together; the Dragon Seal white wine was a most suitable accompaniment for the meal. And she whispered, "To Howard."

Rick echoed the sentiment.

They both used ornate blue and red porcelain chopsticks: Cat ate steamed shredded ham, chicken and pork with bamboo shoots and black mushrooms, while Rick opted for double-braised pork, which he said melted in his mouth.

Halfway through the meal, she put aside her chopsticks and rested a hand on Rick's. "I'm glad you insisted on accompanying me. Eating alone in strange countries in foreign restaurants is no fun at all."

"I'm fun to be with, then, is that it?"

She kicked off a shoe and stroked his ankle with her foot. "You have no idea."

"It's my irresistible charm, I imagine."

"And your modesty, of course." She gently kicked his shin and he made a mock wince.

Then he lowered his chopsticks and peered around fleetingly; nobody was paying them any attention. "Seriously, I'm very concerned."

"I know. I'm driven, but you're aware of that."

He exhaled heavily. "This is a magical place, and it's wonderful to be here with you. I won't say any more about being concerned. I don't want to spoil the moment."

She squeezed his hand. "That's one of the reasons why I love you."

"And the other reason or reasons?"

She smiled. "I'll think of something..."

He displayed a wide grin and lifted his chopsticks, continued with the meal.

They finished with Keemun red tea.

Afterwards, on the way to their room, she said, "I'll phone Yubi after breakfast. As I said, the pair of us have a little catching up to do. Then I'm hoping she can tell me where I can find Dante."

"You're serious about facing Dante?"

"Yes. It must end." She gripped his hand. "I'd like my life back."

"But how can it end? In all probability he ordered the death of your father and my brother-in-law."

"If he shows remorse, perhaps I will let him live."

He glanced around, anxiety on his face. "Jesus, Cathy, you can't talk like that! This is China. The walls have ears."

She giggled. "I was joking." Her eyelids drooped. "Right now, I'm beat. I think I could sleep for a week!"

"Sleep? When we've been apart for so long? We haven't finished catching up—"

She interrupted him with a kiss on the lips. "You have an alternative to sleep in mind?" she purred.

He gave a mock yawn. "I'll think of something."

CAT CAME DOWN to breakfast in a Ted Baker white cotton suit—jacket and cropped trousers—with a red and green floral blouse; she considered that it blended in with the Chinese style; the red Nike air-max shoes finished off her statement. Rick was content to wear a blue polo shirt and cream chinos, with deck shoes.

After breakfast, they picked up their passports: they were now registered with the PSB—Public Security Bureau.

Then they popped out to visit a nearby phone shop —there was no shortage of them here—and bought a Chinese SIM card for both of their smartphones, since the calls would then be much cheaper. Probably monitored, however.

Briefly, they stopped to watch a clutch of Chinese

of all ages in red and blue pajama suits performing tai chi. The display had a strangely calming effect. Nearby in a small park area, several old people sat at collapsible tables, playing mah jong.

On their return to the hotel, they sat in the luxurious foyer, and Cat dialed Yubi's number.

"Yes?" Definitely Yubi's voice. But abrupt. Not like her at all.

"Hi, Yubi, it's me, Cathy. I'm in Shanghai, as promised. Is it convenient for me to come and see you today?"

"Today?" There was a long pause. "Yes, that would be good. Did you have a comfortable journey?"

Very formal. Why is that? "Yes. The usual. An abundance of time to worry about DVT..."

"When can you get here?"

Cat eyed the reception clock. "A couple of hours; it depends on the train..."

"Yes, it would. Good. That is good."

"And then we can talk about Ananke."

"Oh...Ananke... Yes, of course..."

"Yubi, is there something wrong?"

"Wrong?" Another pause, longer this time, then, "No...not at all... Please come quick—" There was a kind of shuffling and then she was cut off.

She turned to Rick. "I don't like the sound of that."

"Maybe she has company—a man friend staying over?"

"When I last spoke to her from Madrid, she was excited and looking forward to us getting together." She pocketed the phone. "Let's go and sort our overnight things. We'll use our backpacks."

41

"Why the urgency? If you're concerned, phone her again."

She shook her head. "No. Something's wrong. Yubi was cut off unexpectedly."

"Probably a bad line."

"No. The line was open even after she finished talking. I heard movement of some sort—"

"You're making me paranoid now, Cathy."

"I told you before, Rick." She sounded irritable even to herself, but she couldn't control the concern that squeezed her gut and crushed her heart. "Yubi worked for my father—and then for Ananke, briefly, before moving here. *She's known to them.*"

"But it's a while since she's had anything to do with Ananke. It can't be connected, surely?"

"That's what I'd like to think. But her address hasn't changed. It's more than feasible that my friendship is on the Ananke file system... Now I'm being paranoid! No organization can be that thorough, can it?"

"I wouldn't put it past them. Why are we still going, if it might be an Ananke trap?"

"Because she's a friend. And she might be in trouble."

Chapter 4

Froglike Cat

Jiaxing, northern Zhejiang province, China

The train journey seemed to take forever, but only forty minutes passed before they arrived at Jiaxing. At the station they hired a cab; Cat showed the driver the address she'd keyed in on her cellphone.

On the outskirts of Jiaxing town, the taxi stopped at a block of apartments.

They got out and she paid.

Cyclists passed in profusion, but not many vehicles. A handful of food-stalls bordered one pathway, each with a trickle of customers, all of whom eyed them both with open curiosity. A woman with a weathered face stood beside a hot drum of sweet potatoes, roasting them; she was as wrinkled as her produce. A side street offered a glimpse of washing that billowed overhead, the line stretched across from one building to the opposite tenement.

They reached the corner. "This will do," Cat said. It was a café, its name printed in Chinese only: Yubi had translated it as *Beautiful Watering Hole*. They went in. Rick wrinkled his nose. Litter and gobs of spittle covered most of the floor. Its beauty had clearly long since faded.

At the counter Cat ordered two green teas; her limited knowledge of the language meant she could only manage simple food and drink orders, and that was all. Then they took seats at a table by the window, overlooking the junction and the road heading west.

The tea was brought promptly by a taciturn waitress.

"*Xie xie*," Cat said and got no response from the waitress, who retreated.

Rick whispered, "I can feel their eyes on me."

Cat gulped the hot liquid. "This isn't like Shanghai —there, foreigners are commonplace, not worth a glance. Here, you're a novelty."

"I've never been that before." He lowered his hand on hers across the table.

"Depending on how long we stay in the country, you might have to get used to it. And get used to being monitored, too."

"Monitored?"

"If we were staying with Yubi overnight, we must register with the local Public Security Bureau."

"Again?"

"Wherever you stay overnight, you must register with the PSB."

"Seems a bit excessive."

She shrugged. "Their country, their rules. Rules are broken, of course."

"I don't like the sound of that. And...?"

"Somehow, I don't think we'll be staying at Yubi's tonight..."

His eyes reflected concern. "Are you sure about this? I mean, shouldn't I come along? For moral support if nothing else."

"No. We discussed it on the train. I'll check to make sure everything's alright first."

"But from what you've said, you don't think it is alright, do you?"

"No, I don't. I'm worried about Yubi, if truth be told."

"Well, then, all the more reason for me to come with you."

She swallowed the last of her tea and stood up, wiped her mouth with the back of her hand. "No, we stick to what we agreed." She hoisted her backpack on her shoulder. "I'll call if everything's alright."

"I know you will." His mouth downturned in disappointment, he stood. "Take care, my love," he whispered and kissed her on the cheek.

They hugged and she left.

She peeked over her shoulder once. Through the window she saw him, sitting with his steaming green tea, his cell-phone on the table. Dutifully waiting. Her heart gave a small leap and then she turned away, hefted her pack, and hiked along the empty dusty road. She'd insisted they travel light—the suitcases could stay in their hotel room. So they'd both shoved in their backpacks a change of underwear and shirt and deodorants; though hers also held a black catsuit and trainers and apparently innocuous extra items that she'd brought through customs without any problem.

Nothing had changed since her last visit. She strolled past a serried rank of apartments, all with connecting balconies; every one identical, thoroughly depressing in their uniformity. Not too dissimilar to the architectural wonders of the Soviet bloc: Communist Deco. She walked on, and soon the pathway came to an end next to a solitary maidenhair tree. She continued along the dusty road, its edges bordered with weeds. Either side of her were fertile fields, the landscape relatively flat. In the distance, several farmhouses built of concrete.

Finally, there it was, as she remembered it from last time. Standing a few hundred yards from the road, a two-story detached house, with the traditional sweeping curves and upturned eaves of its roof; between the columns and beams were brackets, called dougong, cantilevers that supported the structure, allowing the eaves to overhang. The front faced south to gain the most sunlight.

The entrance gates were open, its newel posts crowned with carved pomegranates to symbolize good fortune. The opening was inviting, but she wasn't going to take that route; it was too obvious.

There was a zigzagging gravel driveway leading to the front steps. The zigzag was deliberate, designed to keep evil spirits out, according to Yubi. Cat dearly hoped the zigzag worked its magic.

Parked at the front was Yubi's white Mitsubishi Lioncel, now sporting small hints of rust under the door edges.

A rickety old wooden fence with blistered white paint ran along the front of the property, while the sides were cordoned off with chicken wire fixed to metal posts. A couple of maple trees graced the plot at the front.

The four corners of the house were supported by thick wooden beams, and the first story balcony served as a walkway with balusters, overshadowing a veranda area at the base. Three windows opened onto the balcony walkway; she recalled that there were three more at the rear and one on each side, too.

Sloping out from the base of the upper balcony was a curved roof, its corners adorned with ornate figurines. The upper main roof was a sweeping curvature that rose at the corners, and signified this was the home of wealthy people. She'd met Yubi's parents during her last visit; they had been successful farmers; now they were dead, presumed killed in the missing Malaysian airliner, flight MH370.

The house was really too large for one person. But it was a family home, a repository of memories, difficult to abandon.

Cat continued to walk past the property, glancing occasionally to her left. She noted another car parked on the grounds in the shade of a bushy fig tree: a blue Nissan Livina. Maybe Rick was right and Yubi was entertaining a guest?

A roadside bush offered concealment so she could stop and take time to study the property.

After a while she detected movement in the shadows of the ground level veranda, followed by wisps of smoke. A burning red tip flipped from the shadows and a man stepped down and trod the cigarette into the ground.

She scanned the surrounding area. Nobody worked the fields here, at least at present; yet they looked well-tended. She gripped the metal wire fence and swung herself over, the pack thudding into her shoulder blades as she landed.

Keeping to the edge of the land, she scurried in a crouch along the length of the fence until she reached a large outbuilding; this, she knew, had been used to store farming implements. From here, she had a vantage point to study the rear of the house.

After several minutes, she concluded that nobody guarded this part of the building.

She settled her thoughts, eased her breathing. She knew what she had to do, and now she would do it.

Slipping through the ornate garden and around the pond choking with lotus flowers, all sheltered by magnolia and jacaranda trees, she made for the rear of the house.

Her breathing was steady as she reached a corner of the veranda. She stopped and unslung her backpack and fastened the shoulder straps together, to make a circle. She stood in the circle and looped the straps around her ankles, spreading her legs to make the tough material taut. She raised a hand behind the upright square beam, and the other hand she pressed against the beam at chest level. Then she lifted both legs, frog-like, to gain purchase with the straps pressed firmly against the upright. For ages, men and women had used a similar method to climb palm trees. Once she had established the froglike movement, it was simple to move upwards, shifting her hands higher while her feet took the weight and supplied leverage.

Within seconds, she was beneath the overhang of the lower roof.

Gripping onto the dougong with one hand, she reached down and snagged the strap of her backpack, gently swung it up and over, onto the roof tiles above her. It landed with hardly any sound. She then free climbed round the overhang, careful not to dislodge any tiles.

Now she was on the roof that sloped away from the second story balcony. She heaved in a deep breath, her nerves tingling, her head cocked to one side. Her movements hadn't attracted any attention. She was glad Yubi wasn't living in that block of flats she'd passed on her way here—all identical, overlooking each other. No way could she have scaled that building unseen, since the Chinese liked to stare and were insatiably inquisitive. Not that she was that inconspicuous in her white cotton jacket and trousers with red Nike air-max shoes.

Taking her time, she ascended the sloping tiles and finally grabbed the wooden balustrade and climbed over.

First, she'd see if she could search the upstairs rooms.

Yubi must be in the house, surely? That's what she'd said on the phone, after all.

She returned the straps to normal and slung the pack on her shoulder, then moved across the wooden boards of the walkway, making no sound. She was conscious of at least one man below who could raise the alarm if he heard her up here.

When she came to a window, she peered in with great care, her nerves on edge. She slowly, silently worked her way round from the rear to the front; each room she examined revealed itself to being empty. If her memory served her right, the central window in the front looked out from Yubi's own room. But she needed to check the others, to ascertain if anyone was lurking on this floor. It was quite possible that Yubi wasn't in her room, or even in the house. The fact that her car was parked outside didn't prove anything. Yet, she reminded herself, that phone-call suggested Yubi was waiting for her—or being forced to wait.

Finally, Cat peeked in the front central window, through a narrow gap in the bead curtain. Yes, this was Yubi's room alright. The décor was still the familiar pastel shades, the dressing table comprising drawers and an oval mirror, and alongside it a bookcase containing a mixture of scientific tomes, modern paperbacks by Donna Leon and Michael Dibdin and the five classic translated Chinese books she raved about: *The Book of Changes, Book of Documents, Book of Songs, Spring and Autumn Annals* and *Book of Ritual.* Yubi had always preferred to balance literature with her chemistry vocation.

Cat drew away in alarm and her heart hammered into overdrive.

With her back to the window, a woman sat slumped in an ornate ladder-back chair, her wrists secured by ropes, her head bowed, a white silk gag tied at the nape. She might be unconscious or asleep. She wore a deep blue silk pajama outfit trimmed with red and gold thread; what Cat could see of it seemed unblemished and intact. The hair-style—black, cut short in a bob—and the stature suggested this was Yubi.

Cat studied the sliver of room that was visible,

fearing to detect any movement, any sudden shifting of shadows.

Several tense minutes passed. She believed that nobody else was inside.

Lowering the backpack to the floor, she delved in and retrieved her lock-pick thoughtfully provided by retired cat-burglar Chuck Marston.

She licked dry lips. Time to break in.

Chapter 5

One-Word Questions

Not for the first time she offered thanks to Chuck for teaching her his various house-breaking techniques. The window lock soon opened to her ministrations and she replaced the lock-pick in its purse in her pack. "Never leave anything behind. Always put away your tools as soon as you're done with them," Chuck had admonished often until it became second nature.

She opened the window, thankful that warped wood didn't utter a lament or it didn't squeal on rusty hinges.

Clambering in, she left the window open. That had to be her first choice for a swift getaway. "Prepare your escape route before you do anything else." Another of Chuck's maxims.

Cat froze as she heard voices beyond the room's door, doubtless from the interior landing that she knew ran round three sides of the house and looked down into an inner space used as a dining area. As she stood there, poised ready to flee if the voices approached the bedroom door, she eyed Yubi with concern.

Yubi's left cheek and temple were bruised. She seemed asleep rather than unconscious. She probably hadn't slept much last night, worrying about what might happen today. She was thirty-two but, even now, appeared younger.

The sound of the voices diminished.

Cat breathed freely.

Gently, she shook Yubi's shoulder.

Yubi's smoldering brown eyes started and then she immediately recognized Cat; with such a knowing response, it was doubtful that she'd suffered concussion from that blow to her head, Cat surmised.

"I'll cut you free," Cat whispered.

Yubi bobbed her head.

Using a sharp penknife from her backpack, Cat sliced into the gag at the nape of Yubi's neck.

"Thanks," Yubi managed, licking her lips.

Cat then cut the ropes.

Rubbing her wrists to restore circulation, Yubi whispered, "You came. I did not think you would."

"You sounded in distress. I had to risk it."

Yubi gazed at the open window and her lips curved fleetingly. "It was an easy climb for you, I suspect?"

"A doddle."

"They are waiting for you downstairs."

"I guessed as much."

Yubi stood a little shakily, holding the back of the chair. "Thank you for being here."

"It's my fault," Cat said. "I shouldn't have involved you in this Ananke business."

"I was—I *am* involved." She relinquished the

support of the chair, balled her fists. "Ananke." There was a great deal of anger in that one word. Then she pinched up her face. "They employ people with questionable morals, I think!"

"You can say that again," Cat said angrily. "I saw your car—can we use it?"

Yubi gave a hesitant nod. "I have a spare set of keys in my drawer, here." She went to the dressing table and retrieved a jangling key-ring as well as her cell-phone.

Cat gestured at the window. "We're leaving the way I came—is that alright?"

"Is it safe? I am not a mountaineer."

"Safe enough." Cat offered Yubi a fleeting smile. "Safer than going downstairs and through the front door, I imagine." She tugged the sheets off the bed. "I'm glad they aren't silk. Cotton will be easier to tie into knots." She began twisting them lengthwise and tied one end to another.

"This feels like an adventure from one of my childhood books," Yubi whispered with a grin.

"My favorite was *Mallory Towers*..." In translation, of course. "Right, three sheets should do it." Cat looped the sheet-rope across her shoulder and clambered out of the window. She then helped Yubi get through.

Treading slowly and silently, they worked their way round the balcony to the rear of the house. Here, Cat leaned on the rail to check all was clear. Satisfied that nobody was below at present, she fastened one end of the sheet-rope to the bannister and threw the rest over. It snaked down the sloping roof and the end disappeared over the edge.

"How's the head?" Cat whispered.

"Sore. I'm a little muzzy, but have no fear, I can climb down there."

Cat rested a hand encouragingly on Yubi's shoulder. "Good. I'll go first, to make sure the coast stays clear."

She vaulted the bannister and set her feet firmly on the tiled roof, then knelt and gripped the twisted sheet. Slowly, she walked backward, holding tight, moving hand-over-hand until she came to the lip of the sloping roof. Here, she knelt and, holding onto the sheet-rope, lowered herself over the edge, dangling clear of the wall.

Seconds later her feet were on firm ground. She took a step back so she could see Yubi peering over the rail. She waved to her to come down.

Yubi waved in return and tentatively repeated Cat's actions, though more slowly.

Cat held the sheet-rope steady as Yubi descended the last part, from the lip of the roof.

When Yubi landed, Cat whispered, "Stay hidden in the shadow here. I won't be long."

Anxiety flashed on Yubi's face but she said nothing. Obediently, silently, she slid into the shadows.

Cat slinked round the corner and found the Nissan. Taking out her knife, she removed the cap from the valve stem on the wheel and pressed the nipple in, letting the air escape with a hiss. It sounded very loud, but no sentry came rushing round to investigate. When the tire was flat, she moved to a second tire and deflated that one as well.

Half a minute later, she re-joined Yubi.

"We're going to make a run for your car now. I may have to deal with one of the men."

Yubi looked aghast. "They have guns."

"I'm hoping I can surprise him. Are you okay to drive?"

"I think so."

They reached the corner of the building. The Mitsubishi Lioncel was about six yards away. Cat scanned the veranda and finally spotted the swirl of cigarette smoke, coming from somewhere in the shadows near the front door.

"Go for the car now!" Cat urged in a harsh whisper.

Yubi scampered out, heading for her vehicle.

In the same instant, Cat moved along the side of the building, and spotted the smoker. He was of slight build, wore a suede leather jacket coat, blue cotton trousers, and sported a baseball cap. The smoker noticed Yubi and straightened, then discarded his cigarette. He opened his mouth to yell when Cat landed the heel of her hand on the back of his neck. He grunted and slumped. She followed up with a knee to his chin.

He sprawled backward and fell to the wooden boards.

Her knee hurt—he had a hard chin—but at least he was out of it.

The Mitsubishi engine growled into life.

Cat half ran, half limped to the car, opened the door, slid in, and slammed the door shut. "Go, Yubi!"

She glimpsed two Chinese men emerging from the front door. She committed them both to memory, in case she was unfortunate to see either again. The taller of the two was an imposing man; muscular and broad shouldered, and with a golden complexion, a pug nose, and black hair close-cropped to a bullet-head. His lips puckered above a round firm chin. She massaged her knee. He raised huge hands in a fist and shouted at them. The other one was short, squat with a pencil-thin mustache, a mop of untidy black hair and sunken eyes. This man then spied their fallen comrade and focused on him, while the tall one loped round the side of the building out of sight. He was in for a surprise, she thought.

And then their car had passed the newel posts and jounced onto the main road.

"Yubi, turn right, we need to pick up...my husband!"

"You're married?" Yubi exclaimed. "When did *that* happen?"

"I'll tell you later. He's waiting at the café beneath the apartment block."

"Ah, Beautiful Watering Hole!"

Yubi braked at the curb and Cat waved at Rick sitting at the window. He grabbed his phone and backpack and hurriedly left the café, while patrons and passers-by stared.

"You didn't phone!" he berated as he got in the rear and slammed the door.

"We were otherwise occupied!" Cat snapped. "Belt-up, we're going to be chased pretty soon."

"What?"

"I let their tires down, but they'll probably get after us fast enough..."

"They?"

"Does your husband always ask one-word questions?" Yubi said, taking a left turn.

"Only when I confuse him." Cat turned and

grinned at Rick. "Yubi, meet Rick, my husband. Rick, this is Yubi."

"I gathered that, dear wife. You didn't answer my one-word question."

"They'd tied up Yubi and were waiting for me."

Rick swore under his breath.

"I got her away."

"I can see that, dearest!" he snapped.

Yubi took another turn. "She was marvelous, Rick. Really!"

"I know—she's good at getting people out of scrapes. I'm her number one fan."

"I've never had a fan club before," Cat said with a laugh.

"Don't let it go to your head," he said.

Chapter 6

Bad Driving

While Deshi worked up a sweat on the foot-pump, inflating the second tire, Song paced around the Nissan. He glared at the hapless Enlai who leaned against a tree and nursed his head. Damned idiot! The fool deserved it, though, for hurting the Zhu woman. He doubted if the reprimand he'd given would have any effect. "I set a trap and you let the woman outwit you!" At least, he assumed it was the Vibrissae woman; her reputation preceded her and this one seemed bold enough, tackling Enlai like that. The passport photos supplied by Jabra al-Rashid were accurate; she certainly had altered her appearance. And if that was Vibrissae, where was Barnes?

"Sorry, sir," Enlai moaned. "I was going to stop the Zhu woman from driving off...and the other...she...came out of nowhere... Got me from behind!"

Song spat on the ground to show his disgust, and glared at Deshi. "Haven't you finished yet?"

"Nearly, Boss," Deshi said, panting.

Then Song recalled Laozi's practical advice: *Racing*

and hunting excite man's heart to madness. Yes, he was hunting Vibrissae for Mr. Dante, but he shouldn't let it control his nature. Sobering, he relented and found a first-aid kit in the trunk of the car. He called Enlai over and expertly bandaged the hapless man's head, and then returned the kit to the trunk.

"Thanks, Boss," Enlai croaked.

Ignoring him, Song flexed his fingers and formed a fist, slapping it into his palm as he paced. He didn't believe they'd be able to follow them now: Zhu had too long a lead. It occurred to him that he had a contact who could provide him with the Moreno visa applications, on which they had to state where they intended to visit. But he knew full well that the statement wasn't binding and, already apprised of Vibrissae's deviousness, he was willing to bet that they probably hadn't been open about their true destination anyway.

Based on what Mr. Dante said, Vibrissae's targets were Ananke businesses. Why that should be was never made clear. Her motivation might have proved useful, but for some reason Mr. Dante didn't volunteer that information. There were four Ananke plants that he was aware of, two quite near here—Wuxi and Nanjing; the others were much further off, in Beijing and Datong.

The Zhu woman's Mitsubishi had turned right, heading north, perhaps to the S11 expressway. But where to? Both Wuxi and Nanjing were in that direction. Toss a coin?

AFTER A WHILE, Yubi slumped at the wheel. Cat grabbed it, steadied the car and shook her. "Pull in when you can," she ordered. "I'll take over."

Nodding briefly, Yubi steered toward a section of rough ground, and braked. She put her head in her hands and sighed. "I'm sorry, I'm tired. Exhausted, actually."

"Do you want me to drive?" Rick offered.

"No," Cat said. "I'll take the wheel. Although I haven't driven here, I've been driven, so many of the roads and signs are a bit familiar. Yubi can give me directions."

"Yes, I can do that." Yubi got out, stood by the car and retrieved her cell-phone from her trouser pocket. "But first, I must call Bingren. He has been waiting to hear from us."

"Sounds like he has information," Cat mused, getting out and then slipping in behind the steering wheel.

"He has—and contacts which we may have to use now." Yubi keyed in a number on her phone and spoke briefly in Mandarin, listened, spoke again and then switched off. "We'll meet him in Suzhou. I'll show you where when we get there."

"That was a short conversation," Rick said.

Yubi moved round the car, slid into the passenger seat. "It was probably alright because it was so brief. But you must always be aware that phone-calls can be monitored."

"Blimey. That's enough to make anyone paranoid."

"Didn't you notice the CCTVs in the streets?" Cat said.

"No... Now you have me *really* worried!"

"Don't fret, Rick. We haven't broken any law—yet."

"It's that 'yet' that worries me."

"Me, too," chimed in Yubi.

Without another word, Cat started the engine and pulled onto the road.

Shortly afterwards, she turned onto the S11, and continued to head north, as instructed.

"Is it far?"

"No," Yubi said, "only about an hour away now. Bing's working on a story there, apparently."

Cat checked the rearview mirror and relaxed. Still no sign of the blue Nissan Livina. "Yubi, do you know who those men are?"

"I had not seen any of them before. But I did overhear their names. The big tall one was called Song Chong. The way he dealt with the others, they were obviously his subordinates, which he named Enlai and Deshi. Song was not pleased with the man Enlai who hurt me." She raised a hand to her bruised head and then smiled. "Enlai was the one you knocked out so skillfully. I enjoyed watching that."

Cat chuckled. "Serves him right, then."

"This just keeps getting better!" Rick wailed, hunched in the rear seat.

"There was no danger, Rick. Calm down."

"Yeah, right."

Yubi said, "I'm assuming they all have something to do with Ananke."

"You bet they do!" Rick exclaimed.

Cat glanced across at Yubi. "Did they ask you any questions?"

"No. Song knew you were in the country and expected you to contact me. He didn't threaten to harm me, but he was insistent. Of course I didn't tell him you'd already been in touch. So when you phoned this morning, I was hoping you'd realize I was answering under duress. I had hoped that you wouldn't come and they'd simply go away. A bit naïve of me, I think."

"As I said, I'm sorry you've become involved."

"No need to apologize. But they must want you very much, Cathy."

Rick chuckled. "Oh, they do, Yubi, they do. Very much!"

Cat bit her lip, holding a retort in abeyance. Rick was as nervous as she felt. She'd never driven in China before; she'd always been a passenger. She'd often motored in Europe, so was comfortable regarding the left-hand drive vehicle. Thankfully, the signage on the major roads was in English as well as Chinese characters. There was also the question of a driving license; she knew that foreigners could be given a temporary license, but that entailed attending lessons to study the country's road safety regulations. She prayed they were not stopped by traffic cops and so she stuck to the speed limit, noting with alarm the profusion of cameras. Recalling other visits, she knew that appallingly bad driving was the norm, and insane or suicidal behavior behind the wheel was common, too. City centers and towns would be the worst; it might be prudent if she relinquished the wheel to Yubi when they approached Suzhou.

From time to time, trucks and buses blared their loud air horns as they overtook her.

There was a plethora of bridges; they seemed to be forever crossing waterways; some fields of bamboo, and frequently large stretches of water were seen on both sides; many houses and business premises abutted the waterfronts.

Eventually, she took the S58 turnoff at a cloverleaf junction. It was a looping road, almost dizzying, that turned onto Wudong Road, signed S227. And then they entered a tunnel that took them under a river. The Wudong became the East Ring Road, an elevated bridge affair. She crossed the Loujiang River, and looped off at Guanduli Interchange.

She was anxious as signs passed and found that she had to double back, finally turning onto Qimen Road which crossed Waicheng River. She paid the toll without incident. It had taken them about ninety minutes, but she had the impression of it being much longer, negotiating the unfamiliar roads and signage.

Signs indicated they were entering Suzhou; at the first opportunity, Cat pulled in and Yubi took the wheel.

Cat had been here before, on a tour and, among other places, she'd visited the silk museum and studied a room full of live silk worms, each eating mulberry leaves and spinning cocoons. "If we had the time, Rick, I'd show you the silk museum. Suzhou's been at the forefront of silk production for six thousand years."

"Astonishing," he replied dully. "I'll give it a miss today, if you don't mind."

———

"At last!" Song snapped. The tires were fully inflated. Out of breath, Deshi slumped against the side of the car.

Song got in the passenger seat while Deshi slipped

behind the steering wheel. Enlai sat in the rear, nursing his bandaged head.

"Let's go!" Song barked.

"Which way, sir?" Deshi asked, switching on the ignition.

"Take Enlai and me to the station. We'll catch the train to Wuxi." It was nearest, after all. As they set off, Song pulled out his cell-phone and rang the Ananke plant there and demanded to speak to the head of security. He was promptly put through.

"Yuang here, Mr. Song. How can I be of assistance?"

"You are aware of the alert I issued concerning the two westerners, Vibrissae and Barnes?"

"Yes. I have their photographs posted, and they are on prominent display in the gate-staff's cabin." Some papers were shuffled. "And of course I received your update regarding their use of an alias: Moreno. Have you more information for me?"

"One of them has eluded my men. She may be on her way to your factory. Warn your gate-staff to be especially vigilant!"

"They are always vigilant, Mr. Song."

"Of course they are! How remiss of me." Curb the sarcasm, he told himself. Yuang was only being protective of his staff; it was loyal of the man. *Seek not every quality in one individual,* he recalled from Shujing. "Just ensure they hold her for questioning if she shows up!"

"I will do that, sir."

Song cancelled the call and dialed again, spoke to a contact in the traffic control area headquarters. "My friend, I would like you to do me a favor."

"Tell me, Mr. Song, and I will see if I can comply with your wishes."

"One of my employees has had her car stolen." He reeled off Zhu Yubi's registration number plate. "Can you locate its whereabouts?"

"Yes, I can do that. Do I contact you on this number?"

"Please do. I—and my employee—appreciate it."

He closed the phone.

A short while later they approached the train station and Deshi braked in the car lot.

Song turned to Deshi. "When my traffic control friend traces the Zhu woman's car I'll let you know and you can follow it."

"Yes, sir!" Deshi grinned, as if pleased. To be given so much responsibility was an honor.

PATCHED through from Song's phone, Deshi received details that pinpointed the whereabouts of the Zhu woman's Mitsubishi: entering the city of Suzhou.

He was asked if the driver should be apprehended. Song had been explicit on that issue: "On no account involve the police in any arrest—we want the Vibrissae woman but we don't want to involve the law."

"No, thank you," Deshi responded to the traffic control contact. "Just inform me when and where it gets to its destination."

He estimated that it would take him about an hour to get to Suzhou.

Chapter 7

Lucky Cat

Suzhou

Yubi pulled in at the car lot of the tourist boat pier. They got out, Cat and Rick making sure to bring their backpacks. A street-seller stirred his metal pot of popcorn; bags of his product bulged on the small two-wheel bicycle trailer. People passed, dressed in assorted colored sports shirts. Now, all three of them mingled with several pedestrians and ambled along the canal for a block.

They turned right into Lindun Road, and then left into Dongbei Street.

Trailing behind a small queue of tourists, they entered the Humble Administrator's Garden.

"Why have we come here?" Rick asked.

"Bingren wanted a public place to meet," Yubi said. "We're less likely to be overheard here, too."

"Is surveillance that bad, then?" he said.

"No, it's not bad—so long as you don't indulge in controversial activities."

67

"Like harming a global business such as Ananke?" Cat suggested.

Yubi shrugged. "As long as we don't break the law... This way." She led them along paths through areas of azalea, primrose, gentian and chrysanthemum, some past their season for flowering, and under a covered walkway. Eventually, they emerged on an open paved area that jutted into the lake and provided views of the garden from all sides. According to Yubi, this pavilion and terrace was supposed to resemble the deck and cabin of a boat.

Standing to the left was a man of medium height and build with jet-black hair cut short; he was dressed in a gray gabardine suit. He twisted round as Yubi approached and made a slight bow, palms pressed together. Then he saw Cat and his eyes lit up; the recognition was mutual.

He stepped forward, held her hand in both of his. "Cathy, it is good to see you after so long."

"You haven't changed a bit, Bing," she said, smiling, pleased to see him. "This is my husband, Rick. I'm now Mrs. Moreno." She was really getting used to referring to Rick as her spouse. She wondered if they should make it official. He was a hopeless romantic, after all; he would like that; and in truth, so would she.

"Belated congratulations, Cathy," Bing offered. The men shook hands.

Then Bing said, "I have a keen interest in Ananke, Cathy. But I was surprised to hear from Yubi that you're waging a kind of vendetta against them."

Cat glanced at Yubi, who had the grace to blush, and replied, "It's a long story, and goes back a few years."

"Ah, so. Well, I've been busy investigating Ananke factories at Wuxi and Nanjing," he said. "I've had an interest ever since the Dance takeover of the Vibrissae firm. Naturally, knowing a little more now, I suspect that you have been responsible for a number of embarrassing incidents relating to Ananke, no?"

"You'd be right in that respect," Cat replied. "But isn't this investigation a mite controversial for a state-run newspaper?"

"True, the *Shanghai Daily* doesn't go in for exposés that embarrass the government or authority. This has nothing to do with either; it's a foreign business, after all. And of course I have my own agenda sometimes. I send articles to western periodicals under a penname."

"You're still taking a big risk," Rick said.

"We're not all brainwashed minions of the state," Bing said curtly.

"I didn't mean it like that," Rick replied.

Bing shrugged his shoulders dismissively. "But you are correct in thinking we do have to be very careful." He eyed Yubi. "Is it alright for you to leave your car here?"

"I think so," Yubi replied. "I told old the ticket salesman I would return in a day or so. He said not to worry." She turned to Cat. "Bingren has contacts on the barges."

"That's right," he said. "I think we should go on by barge, rather than road. Particularly now that I know you are being hunted."

"Hunted?" Rick rasped, managing to inject alarm in that single word.

"That is so," Bing replied. "My contact at the Wuxi factory spoke to me not ten minutes ago." He held up his iPhone. "A poster of you both has been released to the sentries at the gate."

"That's a good likeness," Cat observed.

Rick exhaled noisily. "That's it, then. No point in going on. Maybe we can try one of their other factories?"

"No, we go to Wuxi," Cat said, her tone adamant.

"Is that wise?" Yubi asked, concern in her voice.

Bing raised a hand. "Cathy, before you go ahead, I think you should speak to my cousin, Manchu. He works at the Ananke factory. Only then decide on your course of action."

Rick nodded vigorously; and Yubi whispered, "Oh, yes, please consider doing that."

"Alright, Bing," Cat said. "I'd like to meet your cousin."

Rick and Yubi let out sighs of relief.

They retraced part of their route, and came to a landing stage for barges on the Grand Canal. People of several nationalities strolled along the side of the water-way, chatting, taking photographs, oblivious to the world outside their own microcosm.

"Follow me," Bing said, and he led them onto one barge, then crossed to another that was berthed along-side it.

On this second vessel were three people: a small wizened old man, a middle-aged man and a young woman. The younger man and the woman gave a slight nod to Bing, smiled at the others and then went about their business, coiling rope, casting off.

Bing waved at the old man. "This is Sang Ji," he told Cat and Rick. "The other two are his son and daughter-in-law; they live on the barge. They are canal people, the Chuanmin."

Rick said. "Is it okay for us to hitch a ride? We won't get them into trouble?"

"I know Lao, the son, and we agreed a modest price for them to stop here briefly. It has worked well, considering it was arranged at the last minute."

"We must recompense you for that," Cat said.

"Thank you." Bing bowed briefly. "Sang Li's barge has carried 1,000 metric tons of coal south to feed our insatiable industry and are now it is returning north for another load. What with the cost of diesel fuel and canal fees, they'll perhaps make a small profit. The world economy adds to their financial woes. I thought a little extra might help them." He winked at Rick. "Do not worry. They are willing accomplices."

Shortly, the twin diesel engines fired and the vessel joined the busy canal traffic. Sang Li then pushed the throttle full ahead and the engines surged, the propellers biting, adding to the swell.

Oil fumes mixed with the rich stink of animal life on other craft wafted toward Cat. She watched with amusement as Rick produced a handkerchief and held it to his nose.

"The Grand Canal was begun in 486BC," Bing explained, "built by Emperor Yang of the Sui dynasty. It was a brilliant eccentric madness. You see, China's main rivers ran west to east, and Yang wanted to sever this reliance on geography. He wanted to move rice to his court and armies."

"It sounds like it was an enormous endeavor," Rick said.

"And lengthy," Bing agreed. "Its construction

continued for more than a thousand years. No ten-year plan here! About a million workers, mostly farmers, were forced into building the canal. Many villagers starved since there were not enough left to work the fields and harvest the crops."

"So emperors were as bad as communism?" Rick suggested.

Cat nudged his arm and shook her head, discouraging talk of politics, while Bing lifted his shoulders and made no comment.

On either side of them, the canal banks were flush with families, washing dishes or clothes. From time to time they passed tourist boats plying between Wuxi and Suzhou. "The new road systems have taken much of our trade," explained Lao. "Tourism helps compensate, perhaps."

Venerable barges spluttered past, loaded with agricultural produce and factory supplies. There was something appealing and even timeless about trade being plied on the waterways, Cat thought. She hoped it would continue, though wondered at the harsh and uncompromising life the Chuanmin lived.

Shanghai

"Things haven't changed much," Anton Belofsky told Alita as they sat at a restaurant table, the remnants of their meal in several bowls, chopsticks askew. "Marriage by abduction, known as *qiangqin*, still happens here as a result of the imbalanced gender split."

"But our girls are not for marriage," she countered.

"True. It's always about money, though. They say buying a kidnapped bride is about one tenth of the price of hosting a traditional wedding."

"All this talk of marriage—you're not going to propose to me, are you?"

He snickered and then seemed distracted, his attention taken by a Chinese man who had entered the restaurant. Abruptly Belofsky stood and removing his napkin. He waved to the newcomer to join him at the table.

The man was broad and squat with a bald head. Gold rings hung from in his ears and nose. His linen jacket bulged where muscle pressed it taut. His dark eyes glinted, blatantly appraising Alita; she glared back at him, unflinching.

The two men shook hands.

"No names," the man said in measured English tones.

"Agreed." Belofsky gestured. "Please take a seat."

They both sat.

"My contact tells me you want to buy four girls."

"I do," Belofsky replied. "Between the ages of twelve and fourteen, with good complexion."

"And clean," Alita added.

The man eyed her coldly, as if irritated by the interruption of a mere female, and then shrugged and nodded. "It can be done. As it happens, my people have switched to that age-group since the police have cracked down on baby traffickers."

"Good," Belofsky said. "Can you deliver them to the dockside?"

"It can be done. Give me the details."

Belofsky smiled. "With pleasure."

Suzhou

Deshi steered his Nissan Livina alongside the parked Mitsubishi and braked. It was situated precisely where the traffic HQ controller told him. He slid out and locked the car. He looked around at the tourist boat pier and then approached the ticket salesman.

"I sell tickets," the salesman said, unhelpfully. "I don't scrutinize my customers' faces!"

Grimly turning away, Deshi strolled over to a popcorn vendor. "Did you see three people exit from that car?"

"I might have," he vendor replied.

So it was going to be like this, was it? Deshi fished in his pocket for change. "I would like to buy a bag of popcorn."

The sale was hastily transacted.

"A man and two women," volunteered the vendor.

Good! He attempted to contain his excitement. "Did you see where they went?"

"Is the popcorn to your taste?"

Cursing inwardly, Deshi opened the bag, crunched on a handful. He offered a smile, savoring the sweetness. "Good, very good." Though now he was thirsty.

The vendor pointed. "They turned right into Lindun Road."

Peering expectantly, Deshi closed the bag. "Thank you." He pivoted on his heel, intending to head in that direction.

"A little while later," the vendor added to his back, "they returned with another man."

"Oh." Deshi swiveled to face the vendor, clutching the bag, barely containing his rising anger. "And where...?"

"This popcorn will keep. Stay crisp long time."

Taking the hint, Deshi delved into his pocket for more money and forced a smile. "I'll buy another bag. Thank you."

"*Xie xie.*" The coins disappeared in record time. "The four of them boarded a barge that sailed in the direction of Wuxi."

For a fleeting second, Deshi's heart sank. There were only so many landing stages at Wuxi. He must try his luck there. "Thank you," he called to the vendor as he sprinted toward the Nissan.

———

THE BOAT'S little cabin served as the living quarters; there was also a storeroom and of course the pilothouse. On their way, Yubi explained to Bing what happened at her home and named Song as the instigator.

"That is troubling," Bing said. "I had not thought Ananke would resort to such methods. I fear I have underestimated them."

They lapsed into silence.

After a while, Bing broke the quiet and said, "Cathy, how much did you enjoy your expedition to Guizhou?"

"Guizhou?" Rick queried.

"It was before we met, Rick. It was wonderful, actually. Some of the best climbing I'd done, and the views were simply incredible."

"Well, tell us more," Yubi enthused.

"Our expedition was to Getu Valley. The white bullet karst-limestone is ideal for free climbing." She gazed into her memory. "The big attraction is the Great Arch—it's a natural tunnel formed of white limestone about 165 feet tall, 230 feet wide and 450 feet long." She sounded in rapture. "It's formed of dripping tufas, pinches, pockets, and small caves that can accommodate one or two people. It's a great thrill to climb the arch's ceiling!"

"Great thrill?" Rick wailed. "I go queasy just thinking about it!"

"Tufas?" Bing queried.

"Just a form of limestone," she said, "but vast, incredible to see. Admittedly on a much smaller scale, I'm reminded of the ceiling in hall of the Abencerrajes in the Alhambra, Granada, Spain—all those plaster-work stalactites."

"Yes, I can relate to that," Rick said. "I've been there!"

Cat tenderly squeezed his arm and went on, "Young boys scale the cliffs with rope to collect the guano to sell for fertilizer to the many farms in the area. Western climbers only discovered the place about eight years ago."

"Beats staring all day at your game console, I guess," Rick said. "Slow death by computer game."

"Talking of death," Cat went on, "For centuries the local Miao people in the Getu Valley would climb to the top of the cliffs to place the bodies of their relatives there, supposedly to protect them from scavengers. Though the practice stopped a hundred years back, you can still see the coffins."

"Not the kind of view I'd envisage after a climb," Rick said with a shudder.

Yubi giggled.

"It is a part of history, is it not?" Bing said.

"Yes, of course," Rick conceded.

"We have our history here, too, in our waterways," Bing said.

"This is the world's largest man-made waterway," boasted Lao, the new generation of Chuanmin.

Not to be outdone, Bing added, "During the first Opium War, the British blocked the Yangtze, strangling the flow of grain and tax revenues to Beijing." He grimaced. "Within weeks, China surrendered."

"Ah," said Rick, "I read about that! I wonder if drug lords still ply their trade here?"

Bing gave a non-committal shrug again.

A timely interruption occurred as the woman had cooked them a simple dinner of salted fish, rice and stir-fried vegetables and brought it to them.

"Don't refuse it," Cathy warned.

"*Xie xie*," Rick managed, bowing thanks and eating with wooden chopsticks.

Wuxi

Given clearance and passes, Song was driven in the taxi cab through the entrance gate of the Ananke factory. Enlai, still wearing his bandage, sat morosely in the rear beside him, fiddling with his "visitor" lapel badge. The broad drive crunched beneath the taxi's wheels as it veered one way, then the other in a zigzag approach.

The taxi parked at the base of the entrance steps to the two-story office building. Neither of them gave a second glance to the gigantic gold-painted lucky cat, its right paw waving mechanically, that stood to the right of the steps. On the far right was the factory building itself, linked to the office block by an enclosed walkway bridge.

Song opened his door and instructed the cab driver and Enlai: "Stay here. I won't be long." He pinned on his badge and climbed the steps in a loping gait.

The petite female receptionist was expecting him and efficiently led him straight to the security office on the ground floor, at the east side of the building. The door label stated, *Yuang C, Security*. She knocked, opened the door and led him in then left, closing the door after her.

"Welcome, sir," Yuang, the security officer said, rising from his tubular steel desk. He was about forty, tall and slim and appeared smart in his western business suit of gray stripes, a gleaming white shirt and red tie. His eyes were almost black, peering out from pronounced epicanthic folds. He had high cheekbones and his thin lips flickered slightly, possibly in a smile of welcome.

They shook hands across the desk and Yuang said, "Yours is the second visit today, Mr. Song. I hope there are no problems?"

"No, nothing we can't handle, I'm sure."

Yuang gestured at a seat and they both made themselves comfortable.

Song bowed, showing his sharp teeth. "You said 'second visit'—who made the first?"

"That would be Heng. He came by unexpectedly,

enquiring about any visits from Mr. Ying. I found it most odd."

"Odd in what way?"

"Why would the head of security of Nanjing be interested in the activities of the boss of the Nanjing factory?"

"He must have his reasons. I trained Heng, I know he is good. So, were you able to help him?"

"Not much. I've seen Mr. Ying in the offices here from time to time. Calling upon staff members."

"Male or female staff?"

"On each occasion I saw him, he was meeting male staff. He said once that he was drawn to the lucky cat—he believes that it has helped him in his career."

Song frowned. "That doesn't sound like Mr. Ying. I've never known him behave in a friendly manner to any staff... It brings to mind the saying 'You can deceive your superiors but not your inferiors'."

"I wouldn't know." Yuang fidgeted with the blotter on his desk. "I don't believe there is anything...inappropriate in his relations with the staff here, sir. He is a happily married man, isn't he?"

"Yes. With a son, a student in his final year. I must have a word with Mr. Heng, find out why he came by today."

"He left straight after our meeting. But you did not come to discuss Mr. Heng's visit, sir."

"Most perceptive of you, Mr. Yuang, I did not." Song leaned forward. "I have information that needs to be passed to all our establishments in China. I hoped that I could do it from here."

"Yes, of course, I can make all the arrangements."

"I thought so. I read the memo. The surveillance system is recently updated, is it not?"

"Yes. We are very proud of our newly installed facial recognition cameras."

"Good. I want you to feed these into the system." Song handed him the pictures of Catherine Vibrissae and Rick Barnes he had obtained from Jabra al-Rashid, suitably enhanced.

"We can do that," Yuang said. "I will organize the images to be digitized and fed into the system. It will be relayed to the other establishments at the same time."

"Good, very good. Neither of these people may come here, but it's best to be prepared. The fortunate eat food; the unfortunate eat bitterness."

Yuang hesitated, as if wanting to slake his thirsty curiosity concerning the two individuals. Song had no intention of enlightening him further. "Anything else, sir?"

"No. If they show up on the system, contact me on this number." He presented his business card. "Immediately, understand?"

Chapter 8

Waving Cats

Their approach to Wuxi was unexpected and breathtaking. Already there were hints, as the tall buildings emerged from a light mist—or pollution—up ahead; echoing an ethereal Chinese painting. Then as they negotiated a bend in the canal, the great number of skyscrapers and modern buildings appeared to fill the sky. Lao pointed out the restored old houses and other buildings that lined the banks. Attractive arched bridges spanned the narrow waterway, none more spectacular than Qingming Bridge.

Finally, the barge steered alongside the waterfront.

Bing thanked Lao and money changed hands surreptitiously.

Bing, Yubi, Rick and Cat debarked.

Minutes later, the barge cast off and headed into the canal traffic again.

IT WASN'T FAR from the canal to the hotel Cat selected —the Grand Park.

"It seems a mite expensive," Yubi whispered as they entered the immense, gleaming and opulent reception foyer.

"Don't worry," Cat said. "I'll pay—now I can afford it."

"She's come into a great deal of money recently," Rick added. "Sad story. Tell you later."

The reception staff proved efficient; there was no problem as Cat and Rick had their Spanish passports and Cat used her credit card to pay in advance. Yubi and Bing had their resident ID cards.

Rick checked on his iPhone and was surprised at how many PSB offices there were; at least one was close by and they were soon registered.

Yubi and Bing were allocated single rooms while Cat and Rick occupied a double. After settling in and freshening up, they gathered in the Moreno's room. Here, Yubi expressed concern about her car, which she'd left at Suzhou. "I know the ticket salesman said not to worry. But what if Song found it?"

"It's unlikely," Bing said. "He's not a state official, so he won't have access to PSB cameras or reports."

"That might be so, but you can't go home yet," Cat said. "Song or his men might return, or he may have put someone there to watch your house."

Yubi shuddered. "I don't know if I can ever set foot in my home again! And yet it holds so many fond memories."

"I know," Cat whispered, resting her hand on her friend's shoulder, "their invasion of your home seems like a physical violation."

Yubi nodded docilely.

"We'll have to stick together, then," Rick said.

"And," Bing added, "we need to eat soon."

Despite what Cat said, they were reluctant to add to Cat's hotel bill, so they decided to try a restaurant they'd passed on their way.

Once seated in the restaurant, Bing used his phone and contacted his cousin, Manchu.

In thirty minutes Manchu arrived, a stocky dark-haired man in his early forties, of average height with a bow-legged gait; he joined them at the table and complained about foggy conditions outside. Bing translated.

Over the meal, they made arrangements for Manchu to take Cat to the factory the following day: "a fishing trip," she called it.

DESHI HAD HIS CONTACTS, too. A while ago, he'd worked briefly in the Wuxi PSB New Area branch. His contact was amenable to checking foreign nationals' hotel registrations. Deshi was impressed. Within five minutes he had located the Moreno couple registered in the same hotel as Zhu Yubi: the Grand Park.

Licking his lips in anticipation, Deshi telephoned a friend and arranged to meet. He rubbed his hands together, pleased with his progress.

If I can abduct the Vibrissae/Moreno woman, he reasoned then Mr. Song is bound to reward me. That would surely make Enlai jealous, too.

He liked the idea of annoying Enlai at every opportunity.

And he knew someone who owed him a favor. A month or two ago he'd caught the pharmacist selling drugs on the black market but decided not to denounce her; she was grateful. Now she would always be beholden to him; and it so happened that she had access to adequate supplies of chloroform to incapacitate the western woman.

AFTER THE MEAL, as they stepped out of the restaurant into the foggy street, Bing said, "Yubi, Rick, can you make your way to the hotel in this?"

"Yes, of course," Yubi said, eyeing Manchu and Cat. "But why? Aren't you joining us?"

"I don't want too many of us seen together," Bing explained. "The authorities might get curious."

"I'm seriously getting paranoid," Rick said.

"You needn't be," Yubi said, amused. "Despite popular belief, the authorities haven't bothered foreign nationals for over twenty years. That's Bing getting worried about his journalistic credentials being ignored!"

Bing laughed hollowly as they parted.

Shortly, Manchu led Bing and Cat along an embankment of Lake Taihu. Beyond, on their right, loomed above the mist the ugly superstructure and metal domes of a chemical factory. Manchu pointed past that, a dark smudge in the murk.

Bing translated for Manchu, explaining, "That smudge is the Ananke factory. It's been open about a dozen years now. Wuxi New District is one of our country's major industrial parks."

"What do they make here?" she asked.

"Oh, a wide variety of components, sub-systems and equipment. There are in excess of a thousand enterprises registered. A lot of them are international manufacturing operations, too: electronic information, precision machinery, bio-pharmaceuticals, and even new materials. Dotted around the lake there are chemical industries, metal smelting, printing and dyeing—"

"Bio-pharmaceuticals—that sounds like Ananke," Cat said. "They were polluting the North Sea."

"I heard about that. But no, not here; not Ananke." Bing gestured at the lake. "Pollution of Taihu has been an issue for decades. Over a thousand factories were shut by the government and now there are strict monitoring procedures of effluents from those remaining. The Premier has declared war on pollution; perhaps that has to do with the clamor from about seven hundred environmental protection groups!"

"That's good to hear," Cat said. "And presumably the Ananke factory is one of those permitted to operate here?"

"Yes. There's a very important ceramic production industry in this district—making Yixing clay teapots of world renown." Bing chuckled. "Oddly enough, Ananke isn't working on bio-pharmaceuticals. Instead, it's manufacturing ceramics."

"Ceramics?" Cat exclaimed. "That's a big departure for Dante!"

Bing displayed a wide grin. "His second ex-wife is Chinese and she owned the factory at one time until it merged with Ananke. He was besotted with her and went in for everything oriental, such as Daoist gardens, feng shui and fine silk clothing. It didn't last. After his divorce, he reverted to his western culture. She got several millions off him, but he kept the Ananke factory."

"Well," Cat said, "in that case it's probably above-board. What kind of ceramics do they make?"

"Waving cats."

"Did I hear you right? Waving cats?"

"Yes. Fortune cats, lucky cats. They weren't originally Chinese, but Japanese. They call them *Maneki Neko*, which means 'beckoning cat.' The cat has its paw raised as if it's waving in good fortune for its owners."

"Oh, I've seen them—in Chinese restaurants and shops in Spain."

Bing grinned. "That's right. I reckoned you would know about them."

"I suppose there's a story behind the waving cats?"

"Of course. There's a story behind all of our superstitions. One old tale is about a wealthy man who sheltered from a rainstorm under a tree next to a temple. He noticed a cat on the temple steps. It looked like it was beckoning to him, and so he followed it. As he entered the temple, he glanced back just as lightning struck the tree he'd been standing under. Because he believed the cat had saved his life, the man became a benefactor of the temple and brought it great prosperity. When he passed away, a statue of the cat was made in his honor."

"But not the man, the true benefactor?"

"No." Bing lifted his left hand, added, "If the cat is holding up the left paw, this is supposed to attract customers." Then he raised the right hand. "If the right paw is lifted, this invites good fortune and money."

"A wave that doesn't say 'goodbye' but 'hello, happiness'?"

"Yes." He raised both hands and waved them about, much to the amusement of Manchu. "Sometimes you can find a fortune cat with both of its paws in the air; this can also represent protection. A white cat promises happiness, purity, and positive things to come, while a gold one signifies wealth and prosperity. Black wards off evil spirits, red suggests success in love and relationships and a green cat promises good health for the owner."

"Our enterprise is going to need a basketful of lucky cats, I suspect," she said.

Waving goodnight to Manchu, who would wend his way home to his apartment, Bing and Cat began to retrace their steps toward the Grand Park.

The fog closed in.

Cat was barely able to see the tops of the skyscrapers and the many construction cranes that tended to dominate the city.

THE FOG probably had something to do with the fact that there was nobody else about in the street as Cat and Bing approached the entrance to the hotel. Then, unexpectedly two figures emerged from the griseous mist. Their approach was abrupt, so fast, Cat was caught unawares. Her heart leaped as a man charged at Bing and sliced down at him with some implement. Bing let out a grunt and crumpled to the ground. In the same instant, the second man grabbed her left arm and raised his other hand to her face.

Despite the damp grittiness of the city's air-pollution, she caught the sweet smell of chloroform and instinctively drew her head back and slammed her right elbow into the man's face. His grip broke and she followed through with a forceful front kick between his legs. That *always* works.

Her assailant stumbled backward, hobbling and apparently in great pain.

Her pulse raced as she turned, ready to face Bing's attacker, but the man took one look at her, dropped his sap and scurried into an adjacent alley. Her attacker followed, limping badly, and within seconds both aggressors were lost in the murk.

Breathing heavily and coughing on the foggy air, she knelt by Bing, who thankfully was coming round. "Sit still," she told him and took out a small torch from her backpack and shone it in Bing's eyes; his pupils responded, so he probably wasn't suffering from concussion. The sap used on him lay on the ground next to a grubby handkerchief.

"What's that smell?" Bing asked, nursing his head.

She told him, adding that her attacker was naïve, as it was almost impossible to incapacitate someone immediately using chloroform. "It takes about five minutes of inhalation to render someone unconscious."

Rising, she helped him to his feet. He stood, a hand against the building wall, steadying himself. "They wanted to kidnap you?"

"Yes. I recognized him—it was one of Song's men. Deshi."

He groaned. "They must know where we are, then."

"It seems likely. Maybe they have friends in the PSB, after all."

"That's now a strong possibility, one I hadn't

figured on." He massaged the back of his head. "If they know where we are, what do we do now?"

"We meet Manchu, as agreed, tomorrow. Perhaps you can alert the concierge that there is a stalker after me or Yubi?"

"So if anyone asks for our room number..."

"...they'll get reported." She smiled.

Bing laughed. "That idea appeals."

"Don't mention this encounter to Rick," Cat said. "I don't want him worrying."

Brushing dust from his trousers, Bing said, "He has every reason to worry, though."

"Worrying is never helpful, simply debilitating."

Shanghai

Speaking loudly above the din of the air-conditioning unit, Loup Dante said to his secretary on the intercom: "Peizhi, have you arranged my flight to Rome yet?"

"Yes, sir. It is scheduled as you required. And I have taken the liberty of purchasing a suitable gift for Signora Turati."

"Nothing too ostentatious, I hope? She doesn't like 'bling'."

"Sir, I would never contemplate buying such things. No, it is perfume—from the new Ananke collection, Phrygia in a Tantalus set."

He beamed at her, lopsidedly. "An ideal gift, my dear. Thank you for being so thoughtful." The choice was very apt indeed. Gilda had kept him dangling for months before she agreed to marriage. He really believed that this time he would find marital bliss. Perhaps it was her business roots that he found tempting. The difference in age —she was a mere eighteen years younger—did not seem significant. And she came with an heir to her empire, also: Crispino was in his mid-twenties and a useful team member on the board of Turati Industries (Lombardy).

It was not only the merging of minds, but industries. The Turati electronics and chemical plant would prove useful to Ananke. He conceded that she found his business a strong attractant. But she seemed genuinely in love with him, and that felt good. He'd almost forgotten what it was like to love and be loved.

Now, if Song could deliver Catherine Vibrissae and a DNA paternity check could be made, he would at last know if he too had an heir. He envied Gilda that.

Rome

Gilda Turati sat in her black Ritratti underwear in front of her bedroom mirror and powdered her aquiline nose. She deliberately avoided concealing the birthmark on her left temple; it had become the family trademark, resembling a turret. Her long black hair was tied in a ponytail. The evening's sapphire jersey dress lay on the bed. She called over her shoulder, "Mamma, will you be alright while I fly to Shanghai to surprise Loup?"

"Of course, my dear." Her mother walked up to her, rested her hands on her bare shoulders. "We widows can manage very well, I find."

Gilda applied deep red Dolce & Gabbana to her

full lips, blew a kiss to her mother's reflection. "Widow's weeds do not suit me, Mamma. I am too young to be without a man." Loup was putty in her hands, and she would have him.

"You can have any man you like, you know that. Why *marry* him?"

It certainly wasn't Loup's appearance, she mused. He had a pasty complexion and thinning gray hair and the left side of his face had a slight droop, the corner of his eye dragged down, and the skin slightly glossy. He'd told her about that fateful day as a student when he made an awful mistake in the lab and was badly burned. The plastic surgery he received at the time proved to be rudimentary, but he never bothered to correct its shortcomings; strangely, she admired him for that.

"Mamma, he is rich, useful and..."

"...he has a business empire you would like to acquire, no?"

Gilda eyed her mother in the mirror. Mamma's face was lined, her hair gray, yet her chin was firm, her eyes steely. A glare met her. Of all the Turatis, Mamma was the most ruthless, even more than grandfather who began modestly in Turate and built an empire in twenty years.

"He is attractive in other ways, Mamma."

Mamma smirked. "I'm sure he is."

"He has a dangerous streak. I like that in a man."

"Timoteo was reckless rather than dangerous."

Mamma's words stung because she was right. Timoteo was a good lover, a reasonable businessman, but he was a poor gambler. He also resented the fact that his wife retained her family name—"for the business, my dear."

"Have a care, Gilda." Mamma crossed herself. "The Gorettis had something to do with Timoteo's accident, I am sure."

Gilda blinked away an incipient tear before it could spoil her make-up. "I will deal with the Gorettis once I have Ananke..."

Talk of the Gorettis reminded her of Vittorio, her older brother. He'd died in mysterious circumstances. Papa believed the plane crash wasn't an accident, and that pointed to the Goretti family. Despite being saddened by Vittorio's death, she was still happy to take the business reins when her father stepped down, suffering from Alzheimer's. At least Mamma didn't blame the onset of that disease on the Gorettis. Sometimes, she wondered why Mamma harbored such hatred for that family.

"Where are you going tonight, my dear?" Mamma asked. "Not cheating on your husband-to-be already?"

"No, Mamma. It is a business meeting, laying the groundwork for the amalgamation with Ananke."

"Aren't you being precipitate?"

"Loup suggested we merge. He thinks Ananke will swallow us, but he hasn't taken account of our 'extraneous and highly lucrative businesses'. Once we are wed, he will learn what he has joined."

"I would like to see the look on his face when he discovers the truth about the Turati family!"

"I'm sure it will drive him wild with excitement, Mamma."

Mamma pecked her cheek lightly. "I am certain you can control his wildness."

Wuxi

Manchu drove his truck along the road, past blocks of commercial buildings, among them the American Seagate, the Japanese Sony and Matsushita.

Finally, he parked against the curb, a little further along the road, almost opposite the entrance gates, above which was emblazoned in English *Ananke Lucky Cat Factory* and below that. Chinese characters doubtless signifying the same.

Beside the entrance was a security guard's cabin. The place resembled the entry to factories the world over. Cat asked, "Can we arrange for me to visit, posing as a possible buyer?"

Manchu looked askance at her. Bing translated.

Then Manchu shook his head forcefully and let loose a string of rapid-fire words.

"He says you would need valid documentation, and that is not easily obtained at short notice."

Attempting to remove any frustration in her voice, she replied, "If I'm going to look over the place, I need to get in there."

"I am sorry, Cathy. It seems insurmountable. Perhaps you could try another factory—perhaps in Europe?"

"I've come all this way. Bing, with the intention of settling it once and for all with Dante. I doubt if there's anything rotten in this factory—but the files might lead me to one of the others that isn't so clean. He has four in your country, after all. I don't believe all of his businesses are lily-white—it's not like him."

"If you intend to look at their files, you'll need a translator..."

She didn't answer but opened her door, slid out.

Hidden from the entrance gate by the body of the truck, she hunkered down, studied the undercarriage of the vehicle and then straightened up.

She climbed back into the truck's cab. She glanced at Manchu and asked Bing, "You said your cousin works in there, yes?"

"Yes," Bing answered cautiously.

"Would he be able to take you through the gate tonight?"

"I'll ask him." Bing appeared perplexed but put the question to Manchu anyway.

Nodding, Manchu lifted his shoulders and responded in more quick-fire Mandarin.

Bing gave a crisp nod. "It is permitted for family members to visit. He says he would be honored to take me, show me around."

"Good. Then I think we have a way in."

"We?"

"You'll see."

Chapter 9

Dog Meat

Next day, Yubi was happy to show Rick around while Cathy spent time with Bing and Manchu. Rick didn't like being separated from her in a strange country, but he was consoled by the fact that Yubi was good company. The somber thought struck him that the last time he was in good company was in Tenerife and Howard was shot. He dismissed that lurid reasoning with a robust shake of the head. It made a change to behave like a tourist, and there were loads of them about, mostly Chinese. He paid the entry fees for the park and cable car ride.

Firstly, she took him to see Jichang Garden, rich in flowers, shrubs and trees, water features and pagodas of varying sizes. It was so restful he sensed his anxiety for Cathy's welfare diminishing.

Then Yubi took him on the bright red cable car from the park to the top of Mount Hui. The journey in the gondola offered a spectacular view, tree-clad hills and peaks rising ahead.

"It is named the 'kind-hearted hill', Hui Shan," she told him on the way.

"That's what the world needs more of, Yubi—kind hearts."

From the drop-off station, he observed the scene—a stunning panorama of the city and the Grand Canal and Lake Tai. He took several photographs with his iPhone.

Yubi pointed out a seven-story brick and wood pagoda that topped the crest of another hill, Xishan. "Before the cable car, the Dragon Light Pagoda offered the best view over the city."

"I wish Cathy could see this. What a lovely place!"

"You wish to share the view with her, don't you?"

"Yes. But I'll have to settle for showing her these pictures. Unfortunately, she rarely stops to smell the flowers. Too motivated in her vendetta."

"She was always single-minded. Yet it is a useful trait to possess."

"But dangerous, as well."

Absently touching her bruise, Yubi said, "I think she can handle herself well enough."

"She's only flesh and blood, Yubi. I really fear for her when she goes off on her own."

"You love her very much."

"I do."

THROUGH BING TRANSLATING, Manchu provided Cat with the layout of the factory. As they'd observed, there was only the single wide entrance, with a barrier and an office-cabin on the left. "Two security men occupy the office at the gate at night," Bing relayed. "Only one during the day. They take turns doing an inspection of the grounds."

A broad gravel drive swept in, zigzagging no doubt again to avert evil spirits; on the left side of it were ornamental gardens with rocks and plants and ponds; on the right lay the workers' and visitors' car lot. "Manchu will have to park his truck there," Bing explained.

Directly ahead, looming to the right of the entrance steps was a gigantic gold-painted lucky cat, its right paw waving mechanically, inviting good luck and money.

The steps led to the reception lobby and offices of the two-story building, which was linked by an overhead bridge to the factory on the right. Behind the factory was the delivery area for the raw products for the manufacturing process, and the loading bay for the boxed output.

"Even if you got inside, what could you hope to discover or achieve?" Bing asked.

"There may be nothing. In which case, I'll leave the factory alone."

"I would not like to think my cousin would become jobless because of your actions."

"Me neither. If we leave Manchu with the truck parked in the car lot, will you accompany me?"

"I call myself an investigative reporter. I have done this kind of thing before."

"What kind of thing?" she asked, curious.

"Last year," he said, gazing out the cab window, remembering, "I'd been covering a story about a consignment of dogs being transported to restaurants."

"I thought it was now illegal to sell dog meat for food?"

"Just because something's illegal, it doesn't mean people abide by the law, no?"

"True." Indeed, her anti-Ananke activities fell into that category.

"Well, in this case," he continued, "it's *almost* illegal... There's an official clamp-down, but they haven't approved legislation yet, so it goes on. Traditions that stretch back thousands of years are hard to break. Dog meat is considered a popular delicacy as it aids bodily warmth in the winter."

"My God, that is absurd!" Cat exclaimed. "Coats do that more than adequately!"

Manchu gave a strange look, doubtless wondering about the reason for her outburst.

Bing whispered to Manchu, then added, in English, "I contacted a group of activists on my cell-phone and we ambushed the truck, causing a traffic jam on the highway. The dogs were in cages, about five hundred of them, all breeds. Many of them still had their collars and nametags on—they were stolen pets. The group put the healthy dogs up for adoption while the sick ones— and there were a number of those—were sent to pet hospitals in Beijing. Attempts were made to unite those tagged dogs with their owners."

"What about the truck driver and his client?"

"They were helping the police with enquiries when we finally left them."

"I hope they were suitably dealt with."

"Sadly, I doubt it."

"You realize, Bing, that this task is a little different to that? The moral ground isn't quite so firm. And, after all, this is my fight with Ananke, not yours."

"I know the risk of arrest. Our activities could be

construed as a terrorist act. We could face imprisonment or perhaps be shot."

"The police aren't armed, though."

"Well, not until recently..."

"What does that mean?"

"In response to an increase in terrorism offences, last year the government lifted a ban on police guns and agreed to issue the country's police with weapons. My newspaper published a report that showed over eighty percent increase in firearms incidents with police and shootings!"

"Oh, that's really reassuring. Are you sure you want to come with me?"

"Do you read Chinese or speak Mandarin?"

"No, you know I tried but failed dismally..."

"Then, as you said before, you need someone to translate notices and stuff."

"It's the 'stuff' that might prove interesting—I hope!"

"The offices will be alarmed."

"But didn't Manchu say the factory continues to work?"

"Yes."

"The access via the bridge—is that locked?"

He shrugged and asked Manchu, then translated, "He said it isn't."

"Why not?"

He queried Manchu again. "He says the end office is left without an alarm as it has the most recent files, should the manufacturing team need to refer to them."

"I'm surprised, but I suppose if for some reason everything isn't on computer, it makes sense."

HUNCHED OVER HIS OFFICE DESK, Song telephoned Deshi but he didn't answer. Then he rang Enlai: "Have you heard from him yet?"

"No, sir. It's not like him to be so elusive."

"Well, if you hear, let me know."

"Deshi is probably on a wild goose chase, sir. I mean, he is no Sherlock Holmes, is he?"

"You amaze me sometimes. I simply believed that my PSB contact would have been useful and you'd have caught the Morenos by now."

"Deshi got in touch with your PSB contact, sir, not me. I can only surmise. The car might have been traced, sir, but the people we seek might have gone on by train or other means of transport."

"Might this, might that! But gone on where?" Song sighed. "Oh, you're probably right for a change, Enlai."

"Thank you, sir."

Song hung up and bit his lip.

Vibrissae was close, he felt sure.

Foreboding hovered at the back of his mind. The woman's capture should be plain sailing, but it was proving far from that. Mr. Dante had warned that she could be slippery.

He hated the waiting, the enforced reliance on subordinates.

Shanghai

Dressed in a white tuxedo, black silk bow-tie, black trousers and patent leather shoes, Anton Belofsky exuded affluence as he stood beside Alita next to the gangway on the jetty.

The boat was berthed with its stern to the dockside, the gangway sloping upwards, placed in the starboard side of steps.

A couple of hours earlier, he'd paid off his crew; he was quite capable of sailing the *Izolda* to the next port of call. Besides, he didn't want any witnesses to the delivery of his merchandise over the next two nights.

Her arm in his, Alita excited him; not many women had affected him in this manner. She wore a Rosa Clará embroidered skirt-top cocktail dress with silver beading that exposed the deep cleft of her bosom and draped only to mid-thigh. With her free hand, she puffed on a Solaris e-cigarette; this particular vape was odorless, so he caught a whiff of her perfume, Aerin something or other.

His attention was abducted by the sound of a vehicle approaching.

On time, the white unmarked van reversed to the jetty and braked.

The driver killed the engine and stepped out. He was the same broad squat Chinese man they'd met in the restaurant. His dark eyes glinted in the dockside light. "Two tonight, two tomorrow," he said in a husky voice. "Cash on delivery."

"That's the deal," Belofsky said. "Do you want any assistance?" He hoped not, he wasn't dressed for any kind of manhandling.

"No, I have my people." The driver opened the rear door of the van. Two men crouched inside; they could have been the driver's brothers; they all looked alike, though didn't sport any gold jewelry. "Family," the driver said, in confirmation.

The driver scanned the waterfront—nobody was about in the vicinity—and then gave a sign to the two men. Both moved into the shadowy innards of the van and then emerged, each carrying a long bundle of opaque polythene over his shoulder.

Belofsky sensed Alita's breathing rate increase and studied her. Her chest heaved against the embroidered fabric as she watched the men carry their loads onto the gangway.

"Would you like to make them comfortable while I pay the driver?" he asked her.

She peered at him, her eyes alight in anticipation. "Yes, I would, dearest." She disengaged her arm, and pitched the e-cigarette into the river.

"Aren't those things re-usable?" he asked.

She shrugged. "I can afford a new one every time," she said and hurried after the two men and their burdens. Neither man had any difficulty stepping onto the main deck.

Beckoning to the driver, Belofsky delved into his inside jacket pocket and produced a bulging folded foolscap brown envelope.

The driver took it and slit open the flap, his slick fingers expertly counting the bank notes. He nodded, satisfied. "Same time tomorrow?"

"That would be good, yes," Belofsky said as the two men returned and descended the gangway.

Waving them off, Belofsky swung round and climbed the gangway.

He went below to the cabin deck and found Alita in the first cabin at the other side of the double bed.

The polythene sheets lay crumpled on the carpet. Sprawled upon the bed were two Chinese teenage girls, dressed in identical sleeveless cheongsams fastened by frog buttons, their lithe bare legs exposed at the side-slits.

As agreed, they were drugged. It made life much easier, until they acclimated to their new role in life.

Alita leaned over, fingered the mandarin collar of the nearest girl. "Silk brocade," she said, eyeing him. "Exquisite. The chrysanthemum pattern suits their pale complexion."

"The chrysanthemum pattern is supposed to signify a noble mind, but it won't be their minds that will earn me all that money, my dear."

"I know." She reached across to the bed-head, pressed a button and a small compartment opened. She extracted a shackle and fastened it to the girl's right wrist. She rucked up her skirt, clambered onto the bed, straddled the girl, and pressed another button, releasing two shackles, which she fixed to this girl's left wrist and the other one's right.

"You enjoy this, don't you?" He knelt at the foot of the bed and attended to the girls' ankles with another series of shackles.

"Yes, I do."

It was a power-trip for her. She was so like him in many ways; that was one of the attractions.

As Alita scrambled over the second girl and secured

the left wrist, she added, "They'll get a shock when they come to. Will you film them?"

"I'll have to, since we won't be here to witness it, and I know how much you like to watch their reactions."

He stood up, brushed the knees of his trousers. "Cocktail parties are a necessary chore in my business. And of course there is the symposium tomorrow night; that is where the real business can be found."

"Why do you carry on? It's not as if you need the money."

"What do filthy rich people do with their time, eh? Squander it on the gratification centers of the brain, no?" He wrapped his arms round her, pulled her tight to his chest. "And you gratify me so well, my dear."

She squirmed, exciting him. "Do we really have to go for cocktails?" She pouted.

He kissed her savagely, and then sharply pushed her away. "Yes, my dear." He held her at arms' length. "It's a jungle out there. If I'm not seen to be keeping a finger on the pulse, my business and riches could hemorrhage in no time. Many men—and a handful of women—are only waiting for me to relax, to go soft..."

"No risk of that," she said with a smirk.

Chapter 10

Qigong Training

Wuxi

As she hung there, Cat was glad Rick hadn't come with her; he'd have had a blue fit if he knew what she was doing. Right now, he'd be fretting in the hotel bar with Yubi. At least she didn't feel too guilty; the pair had said they'd had a good time earlier, sightseeing.

She was dressed in her black catsuit and black trainers, the backpack tightly strapped to her shoulders. Her hands gripped a cross-member of Manchu's truck chassis, staying aft of the gearbox and to the driver's side, away from the exhaust. Extensive bouldering and free rock climbing had equipped her with strong hands and wrists, at least. Her feet rested precariously on the back-axle casing, while the backpack and her buttocks were mere inches from the road that sped beneath her.

Hot air from the engine casing combined with the heat of the exhaust whipped over her. Choking on dust and the fumes of grease and oil, she clamped her mouth tight shut and hoped the raucous noise of the vehicle would soon desist. She should have obtained a medical face mask, she supposed, but at such short notice she couldn't obtain one.

She recalled a Chinese saying: "Falling hurts least those who fly low." Trouble was, she was flying low at about forty miles per hour.

Hang on!

Not for the first time, she wondered why she put herself at risk like this. She'd hurt Dante quite a bit already. Nothing may result from tonight's jaunt. It could be a waste of time. Or they could all get arrested. For what? To repay Dante, of course! There were other ways, surely? Hire an assassin—though God knows how she would go about doing that. She'd met a fair number of shady characters during her fashion shoots, one or two capable of supplying her with a weapon, but never had she encountered a hired killer—as far as she knew. Would paying an assassin give her satisfaction? No. She wanted Dante to feel pain, to grieve for what he had lost —slices of his empire gone—and know she was responsible.

She was appalled that she could ever contemplate killing the man, no matter how much she hated him. What was she turning into—a vile creature like Dante? Was it an ego trip? Rick virtually implied that more than once, the besotted darling. He was a pragmatist and realized that she could not go on indefinitely cheating the odds while making life uncomfortable for Dante. At some point, if she continued with her crusade, she had to admit she would meet with an insurmountable problem, awful repercussions or—heaven forbid—a fatal disaster.

Abruptly, Manchu braked and the truck shuddered to a halt. The juddering stop jarred her whole body, her left foot slipped and the sole slapped the ground; the hiss of the air brakes covered the sound. Her heart hammered as she hastily strained her thigh muscle to lift her foot and wedge it firmly.

She presumed Manchu had stopped at the entrance gates. She hoped that the gate staff didn't use sniffer dogs or under-vehicle inspection mirrors; at least her reconnaissance earlier in the day suggested they didn't. But now it was night, maybe their security procedures would alter subtly and be tighter.

AT THE GATE, the sentry stepped out from his cabin and strolled round the truck, taking his time, giving its interior a perfunctory check. Bing hoped the man would hurry up; he could imagine that Cathy's fingers might be holding tight right now, but he feared that the tendons in her arms would be straining.

Manchu explained that his cousin was along for the ride; he took his time in the telling, too, blast him.

"You need a visitor's pass," the sentry said.

Great! More delay. He hoped Cathy didn't relax, get tempted to lower herself to the ground, rest her forearms and then reposition herself. Bing shifted in his seat, listening. He peered at the wing mirror but couldn't detect any sign of her feet or moving shadows. *Hang on, Cathy!* He found he was gritting his teeth.

Finally, the sentry came out, brandishing a clipboard. "Sign."

Bing signed, returned the clipboard.

"That's fine. Here's your badge." He asked Manchu, "Where are you going?"

"Loading bay. Delivering tea." Manchu patted a box wedged between the dashboard and the windshield.

"Ah, they always seem to be drinking tea! The night-shift is so lazy!"

"When is your tea-break?" Manchu asked.

Get a move on! Bing wanted to shout, fearing Cathy would lose her grip any second now. His insides churned. If Cathy was caught, he would be too, and then his career might end tonight.

"I get relieved in an hour." The sentry went into his cabin and then the barrier was raised.

Bing held his breath as they drove through, hoping that Cathy wasn't visible to the sentry.

Manchu steered along the zig and zag road.

Bing studied the wing-mirror, expecting to see Cathy tumbling behind them at any second.

He breathed a little easier as a small grassy knoll now hid the car lot from the gate cabin.

Manchu parked the truck, brakes hissed, and he switched off the engine.

Bing released a huge sigh, opened his door and clambered from the driver's cabin.

———

Cathy let go, dropped gently onto the tarmac and rolled out from under. With aching arms, she brushed herself hastily as Manchu climbed down.

Without a word, Manchu tucked the big box of tea under his arm and swayed from side to side as his bow-legs made for the loading bay area, to the right. He didn't look back.

"Are you alright?" Bing asked. "I felt for you. The blasted gate sentry took his time!"

"Yes, I'm fine." She passed a hand over her face and it came away grimy and black. Probably grease from the undercarriage on her hand as much as on her face. "I don't know how much longer I could have held on, though." Climbing, she rarely had to hold herself in one position for so long. Movement, changing stance was key to preventing any muscle freeze. She massaged her forearms. "My muscles feel a little weak." A familiar feeling she'd experienced dozens of times while climbing. "The strength will return shortly," she added and scanned the buildings.

She could try to sneak into the factory at the loading bay end. But she was interested in that office with the latest files.

There was a light on up there, and it percolated onto the covered bridge; more light shone from the narrow high windows of the factory and spilled from the loading bay section.

A drainpipe ran down from the gutter of the roof of the enclosed bridge. She climbed this with ease. Reaching the adjacent window of the bridge, she took a tool from her backpack and jimmied open the latch. Sinuously, she slid in onto the firm floor of the bridge.

Bing followed, more slowly, and she helped him get through.

She closed the window and then they both stood and listened.

Nothing nearby untoward, she reckoned. She

moved to the left, heading for the open office, an oblong of light shining onto the floor of the bridge.

They entered the office. There were four aisles of filing cabinets; directly opposite was a door, which was locked; beside it on the wall, a key-pad. Cat wiped her hands on her pants and then checked the first filing cabinet, nearest to the bridge door; it was unlocked. The files inside were in Chinese, obviously.

"I don't know what I was expecting to find," Cat whispered ruefully. "I've been a fool. I can't understand any of this!"

Bing joined her and gave the files a cursory glance. "That's odd."

"What?"

"There's a date here for tonight's manufacture output. It's destined for Tenerife."

"What's so strange about that? They have plenty of Chinese shops on the island. Spain's riddled with them."

"Yes, but the allocation is different." He riffled through other files. "The others from yesterday and all of last week, they don't have a special marking like this one: see."

He was right. It was a rubber stamp in deep red ink, like a rose or other flower. Yet none of the other consignments he showed her carried this stamp. "Can you check back further?" she asked.

He did so and extracted another folder. "This is the same—also for Tenerife."

"Are there any other consignments for Tenerife?"

"Yes, two others—but they don't carry this mark."

Cat used her phone to photograph the latest

consignment's paperwork. "We'll check this later. Let's go."

"Wait," Bing urged in a low tone.

"What?" Cat whispered.

"Listen!"

She paused and her pulse-rate grew rapid. Somebody was striding along the bridge.

They silently closed the filing cabinet and rushed to the other side of the room, behind an aisle of cabinets. She heard Bing's breathing, made calming motions with her hands. He acknowledged her admonition, closed his eyes and seemed to relax, as if going into a trance. Qigong training, maybe. She adopted similar calming techniques when free climbing, learned from an Englishman who ran classes in Inverness.

A stocky man in overalls entered the office and went straight to the cabinet they'd opened. He fished inside a folder, removed the sheet Cat had photographed seconds earlier. He scanned the page, nodded and went out, taking the consignment sheet with him.

Letting out her breath slowly. Cat stood up, Bing beside her.

"I'm curious," Bing said. "Let's follow him."

The man had gone through the far door at the other side of the bridge.

Tentatively, they both crossed the bridge and stood at the door, listening.

There was a great deal of shouting and the whirring of an engine.

Cat unslung her backpack and removed her lockpick; she soon opened the door, then slid through the gap and found herself on a walkway, a landing that overlooked the right side of the factory—the end of a production line. There was a freight container, its metal doors open. Pallets laden with boxes were being moved by forklift on the slight ramp into the gaping maw of the container, driven inside and lowered. Then, without its load, the forklift reversed out. The boxes were stamped with *Fragile, Ananke* and *Lucky Cat*. To one side of the container was a reach stacker, which would be used to load the container onto a flatbed truck when ready.

A hooter sounded; it sent her heart pounding in alarm.

All activity seemed to stop at once. Chatting together, the workers unhurriedly left their posts and moved to the left of the factory, and went inside a covered area with frosted glass windows. Then Manchu emerged from there and sauntered toward the loading bay exit.

"Tea-break?" Cat guessed.

"Tea is essential to work harmony," Bing whispered.

"How long do you reckon they will take?"

Bing shrugged. "Maybe thirty minutes."

"Right." She moved to the corner of the walkway. Hooking her insoles against the ladder sides, she slid down. Manchu had gone by the time she soundlessly hit the floor.

Bing followed, descending much slower, using the rungs in normal fashion.

Cat made a mental note of the container's identification number: C-WX-LC44—manufacturer code, the ownership code, and usage classification code.

She went inside the container, which measured about forty-eight feet long, nine feet high. Already, about half of it was stacked with identical boxes. She moved to the side, squeezed in a small gap, and slid her knife in the sticky-tape seal, opened a box. Inside amidst polystyrene balls were six gold-painted lucky cats; there were probably six more under them. She took one out; it felt heavier than she'd expected; she gave it a shake. Nothing moved. Carefully, she used her knife to break the ceramic cat, dropping the shards into the space in the box. Inside the cat were three hard dark brown solid cakes wrapped in cellophane. She put one of them in her backpack and returned the others to the box, hiding the broken pieces and two packs under the top layer of cats. Hastily closing the lid, she hid the box under another from the stack.

Anxiously, Bing whispered, "What have you found?"

"Raw opium."

"Are you sure?"

"I'm a chemist."

He swore.

"Let's get out," she said.

They made their way down the ramp of the container. The loading bay was to their right—not visible to the workers in the tea-break cabin area.

Bing walked hurriedly through the loading bay doorway, Cat following.

Too late, she noticed a CCTV camera sited above the opening, and her heart seemed to sink into her stomach. "Quickly, get to the truck!"

She ran and caught up with him. Together, they rounded the corner of the factory building, dashed along the raised loading bay section, skipped down stone steps and raced across the tarmac toward the car lot.

Manchu had moved the truck and its hood was now pointing at the broad drive.

As before, Cat slid under the truck, grabbed hold and then banged her foot on the undercarriage to indicate she was ready.

Manchu fired the engine and they drove along the broad drive. Over her shoulder she fleetingly glimpsed the giant lucky cat waving goodbye to her.

Chapter 11

Papaver Somniferum

Wearing only his boxer shorts, Song lay on the top of his hotel bed, propped up against two pillows. He was reading an English translation of *Monkey* by Wu Ch'êng-ên. It was his favorite book so he compromised, finding it useful to read it in English to maintain and even increase his familiarity with the language.

His cell-phone vibrated on the nightstand. He answered it.

It was the security officer, Yuang. "Sir, the woman you alerted us about was spotted in the loading bay at our factory ten minutes ago."

Ten minutes! He sat up, swung his legs over the edge of the bed. "Ten minutes? Why was there no alarm?"

"The facial recognition system is not linked real-time to the alarm system yet. However, it has flagged us that she was there."

"Ten minutes is a long time where crime detection is concerned."

"I know, sir. I've ordered a shut-down at the gate and personnel are checking the current load to see if anything is missing."

"Very well." He was a competent man. *He who has not faith in others shall find no faith in them*—Laozi. "I need a record of whoever has entered or left that establishment in the last two hours. I will be there in half an hour to review your results."

Shanghai

"Hi, Daphne!" She was waiting for Gene in a rear corner of the coffee shop. He walked to her table. She stood, looking attractive in a western style gabardine jacket and trousers, and yellow silk blouse. They shook hands and then sat. He couldn't place her age, and had no file on her; she was perhaps in her early thirties.

Tan Daphne had told him she was originally from Singapore but had worked in Shanghai for ten years, four of them as a spy for CITES. She had high cheekbones, black hair cut in a bob, and pearl teardrop earrings.

She smiled, her lips thin, mouth quite wide, and her dark eyes glinted in the light.

"I came as soon as I could," he said. "Do you want another coffee?"

"No, thanks." She glanced to left and right, and he idly followed her gaze.

Nobody was interested in a meeting between a local and a westerner. The denizens of Shanghai were used to seeing all nationalities and prided themselves on their cosmopolitan attitude.

"I had the impression it was urgent we met," he said.

"It is." She bent and lifted from the floor a raffia shopping bag. "Inside is the video of my last contact. You need to get the authorities to act fast. The merchandise is going through the docks tonight."

"My dockside contact is Mr. Kuang. You had no trouble getting this, then?"

"No. If I had, I wouldn't be here, Gene. I'd very probably be fish food by now."

He studied the bag. She was right, of course. She took an immense risk whenever she posed as a potential business contact or trader. "You'll also find my contact has revealed a good deal about his business practices—source of supply, delivery route, customs evasion contacts."

"That's good work, Daphne."

Although he'd only known her a couple of days since he landed and made contact, he liked her. He'd been due to come here anyway, but the process was hastened when he was asked to replace Jepson who went sick with food poisoning.

Normally, it wouldn't have been critical, but Daphne had been working on this particular contact for two months and was ready to reel him in. Timing was everything. So he'd got the call while in Tenerife.

They stood at the same time. He paid and they left.

She led him to her parked car and drove him to a nondescript office in a modernistic block. She let herself in and he followed. The place was unoccupied. "It has been purchased by a shell company. It isn't only the Chinese who indulge in this kind of chicanery."

Gene nodded. "I know." He was aware of similar goings on in London and New York. Multiple property purchases where the new tenants never seemed to appear—in daylight, at least.

She knew her way around the place which was crammed with a wide assortment of machines. "It won't take long, since the system's digital," she said. Calmly, competently, she copied the video images, made DVDs of them, and also copied everything to a memory stick.

"Is the computer secure?" Gene asked, pointing to the black tower on another desk.

"Yes."

He shoved the memory stick into the computer tower's USB slot, tapped away on the keyboard and accessed his own email account. In a few moments he had emailed the contents of the memory stick to the Chinese officer who was waiting for his message.

"He won't take long, I reckon," Gene said.

He wasn't wrong. The response by email was almost immediate.

He beamed at Daphne. "That's going to happen in about an hour."

"Good." She let out a sigh of relief. "Two months cultivating that swine; and now he will be put away. You know, that feels good."

Wuxi

They gathered in Cat's hotel room. She'd taken a swift shower to get rid of the oil, dust and grit and now she sat on the bed alongside Rick. Bing and Yubi occupied the two chairs.

"What made you suspicious?" Bing asked.

Cat held up her cell-phone and showed them the image on its screen. "The rubber stamp—it's not a rose but a poppy pod, *Papaver somniferum*."

Yubi looked at it. "Isn't that a bit foolish of them to draw attention to an illegal product?"

"I suspect it's only for internal identification."

"I agree," Rick said. "They won't use it for bills of lading or other legal documentation. Most of their consignments will be legitimate. But they definitely need to know which contain the opium."

"It seems this is a reversal of the old Opium Wars," Bing mused. "Now, somebody in *Ananke China* is addicting the west..."

Cat stroked her chin. "I'm surprised that Dante is involved in drug trafficking, though."

"Perhaps he is blissfully unaware?" Yubi suggested.

"There's nothing blissful about Dante," Rick said feelingly.

SECURITY OFFICER YUANG pointed to the CCTV image on the screen: the truck's yellow license plate showed clearly. "There, you can see it."

Song showed his sharp teeth, on this occasion a sign of pleasure. "And you can trace it?"

"One moment." Yuang moved to the computer keyboard and typed in a string of letters, used the mouse to click on a series of drop-down windows, and finally pointed: "It's registered to Chang Manchu." Another click, and he was presented with an address and considerable data from personnel files.

"So he lives near here, then?"

"Indeed," Yuang said. "Do you want to accompany me?"

"Yes. I'd appreciate being in at the kill." In truth, as Yuang's superior, he could easily insist; but it was all about "face". Allow Yuang the illusion of authority.

Yuang grinned briefly. "I thought you would."

Song pulled his cell-phone from a pocket. "I'll bring along my man Enlai." It was not a request.

"Of course."

Sleepy and unkempt, Enlai joined Song in the back of Yuang's limousine and they set off for the apartment block where Chang Manchu lived with his wife and son. Family: always worthwhile leverage, Song mused.

When they got there, they tumbled out. Song was alert, and scanned the street.

Security officer Yuang went first, entering the vestibule. He indicated the door. The Chang Manchu apartment was on the ground floor.

Enlai pounded a fist forcefully on the door.

Song pointed to the doorbell and raised an eyebrow in enquiry.

Enlai shrugged. "A knock is more imperative, sir. Makes them anxious. Believe me."

It didn't seem so to Song. After a lengthy interval Manchu answered, holding the door only partially open. "Yes?" Manchu said in an unwelcoming tone. He didn't seem anxious.

Song stepped a pace in front of the others. Glimpsed behind the employee Song could see the hallway, which was painted a dull brown, the floor covered by green tiles, but there was no inquisitive family in evidence. He couldn't hear any television, radio or any other electronic equipment, either. "Mr. Chang?" he enquired, even though he recognized him from the computer's personnel file. Stand by formalities.

"Yes?" Manchu squinted, eyes betraying alarm at sight of Enlai's bandaged head. "Who are you and what do you want?"

"My name is Song Chong and I'm head of Ananke security." He flashed his ID. "I need to talk to you now, Mr. Chang."

Manchu paled. "Eh?" Now he was anxious. "What's so important you must call at this time of night?"

"Manchu, it *is* rather urgent," Yuang explained, standing behind Song.

"Ah, Mr. Yuang!" Relief showed on Manchu's face. He moved aside, opened the door wide. "Come in." He gestured along the hallway. "Please go into the kitchen. At the end."

He shut the door and followed them.

They stood awkwardly in the small room, next to a Formica-topped table and two chairs, as Manchu entered.

"Are you alone?" Yuang asked, his pelvis resting against the counter.

Manchu nodded. "My wife and son have gone to her mother's for a day or two."

Song said: "Enlai, please go and check."

"There's no need," Manchu said as Enlai left the room.

"There is," Song grated. "Please sit down, Mr. Chang."

Cowed by Song's tone, Manchu sat.

Minutes later Enlai returned. "The place is empty. There's nobody else here." He moved to stand with his hands resting on the back of Manchu's chair.

Song smiled, showing his sharp teeth. As expected, Manchu recoiled at sight of them. "Now, Manchu, tell Mr. Yuang why you went to the factory tonight."

Manchu gave the impression of being intimidated, with Enlai virtually breathing down his neck. "My cousin, Bingren, he has pestered me for a long time. He wanted to see the factory."

Song pulled up the other chair, reversed it and sat, leaning on the ladder back. His tone was firm, but not threatening. "The workers only remember you—delivering their box of tea."

"Yes." Manchu gave an enthusiastic nod. "That's right."

So eager to please, Song thought. Too eager? "So why didn't your cousin go with you to meet the workers in the factory?"

"Bingren is a bit shy around strangers..."

"Your cousin is a journalist, Manchu." That exposal widened Manchu's eyes; he must be wondering how much I know, Song mused. "I don't think journalists are shy people, do you?"

Manchu lowered his gaze to the floor.

Enlai gave a slap to the back of Manchu's head. "Answer the boss!"

Yuang stepped forward, exclaimed, "There is no call for that kind of behavior."

Song gave a curt nod. "You are correct, Mr. Yuang." He eyed Enlai. "I have already had to chastise you for acting rough. I trust I will not have to do so again. Now, let Mr. Chang gather his thoughts."

Rubbing his head, Manchu stammered, "Bing— Bingren looked around... honestly, that is all. While I ... while I was chatting to the men and...and drinking tea."

"Your cousin didn't want any tea, then?"

"No...it is his bladder..."

Enlai slapped him again. "Don't get funny with the boss!"

"Enough!" Song barked, holding up a hand. "My friend Mr. Chang is trying to help us, I'm sure. Is that not so, Manchu?"

Feverishly now, Chang Manchu whispered, "Yes," his eyes plaintive. "When we left, some minutes later, Bingren said he was very impressed. He will write a good article about the lucky cats' production in his newspaper. That should help business, I think."

"My business is security at Ananke establishments," Song grated. "If your cousin wanted to write about the factory, he should have approached our public relations office and obtained permission."

"I am sorry. I did not realize. It is not as if anything is top secret."

"Ananke has business competitors who might take advantage of information gleaned from a visit such as your cousin's."

"I am disappointed in you, Mr. Chang," said Yuang. "We must guard against industrial espionage."

"Yes," said Song. "That is why we have CCTV cameras."

"I—I'm sorry... I did not think..."

Song leaned forward, his face close to Manchu's. "What I find puzzling is that the camera at the loading bay showed your cousin leaving the factory but not entering. Can you explain that?"

Manchu bit his lip, squinted. "No, I cannot. It's all a bit technical to me..." He winced as Enlai leaned on the back of his chair. "The gate sentry...he took his visitor's pass off Bingren, logged him out. Everything was normal. I remember that distinctly. Was there a camera at the gate? That would show, wouldn't it?"

"Yes, we know he left with you." Song glared. "Did you see a woman?"

"Well, yes," Manchu said quickly, too quickly, "four of the production line workers are women."

"*This* woman!" Song snapped, shoving a sheet at Manchu.

Looking at Catherine Vibrissae's photograph, Manchu said, "No, sorry, I have not seen her. She is not Chinese."

"Of course she isn't! Look again, man, and study her face!"

Grimacing as Enlai shook his chair, Manchu replied, "I think," he croaked, "I think I would have noticed—she is a westerner, no?"

"Most observant of you, Manchu. Very well." Song scowled, signed for Enlai to desist. "For now, you are under warning. Tread with great care."

Nodding briskly, Manchu said, "Yes. I will approach public relations next time."

"Make sure there is no 'next time', alright?" Song

stood, towering over Manchu, huge hands balled into fists.

Manchu gulped. "Yes, sir. No 'next time', sir, yes sir."

Yuang said, "I'll speak to you tomorrow, Chang Manchu."

"Yes, sir," Manchu said, eyes downcast.

"Very well." Song swung round and made for the door, with Yuang by his side. He stood waiting and eventually Enlai rushed forward to open it for him.

They stepped onto the street.

So close to catching her! He fumed as they got to the car. What did she want?

The merchandise didn't appear disturbed. And we know she didn't travel in that truck; and she didn't leave by the gate.

She must have scaled the fence without being detected by any of the other cameras. That was quite an accomplishment.

She was formidable, he had to admit.

He was surprised to find that he harbored a grudging respect for Catherine Vibrissae.

Chapter 12

Single-Minded

Shanghai

Gene appeared relaxed and yet business-like, Sara thought, admiring him as he talked to Mr. Kuang, the port authority man in the office that overlooked the dockside. Gene wore a Corte Inglés blue cotton shirt and beige Barbour chinos, with Emidio Tucci brown leather shoes, apparel she had selected for him in Tenerife. The standard fan blew cool air at her, wafting her blue Punt Roma tropical print dress. She adjusted the strap of her shoulder bag and listened and observed.

The room was filled with Chinese men and women in regulation shirts sitting at computer terminals; their backs and under-arms showed sweat marks that blemished the white material. A couple of them were talking rapidly on the phone. She'd encountered Chinese conversing in their own language in their shops and restaurants in Spain, but found they tended to speak faster and louder here; it was mind-blowing. Despite being a linguist, she realized she'd never master Mandarin.

Suspended from the ceiling was a TV screen that showed shipping and boat traffic for the river, and berth numbers. Idly, she studied the screen.

She stared.

She swallowed.

Among a handful of others, the *Izolda* was listed and in the owner column was the entry *A. Belofsky*. She recalled with unwelcome vividness Howard Greenleaf being shot in Santa Cruz. Her flesh felt chilled. The Guardia lieutenant had said that Anton Belofsky was responsible for the murder of his fellow officers and probably also Howard's death. Should she mention it to this official, Mr. Kuang? He would make inquiries and perhaps they could apprehend Belofsky and get him extradited to Spain. No, be sensible, she chided herself. There may be masses of people with the name of Belofsky. It might be as common as Smith in England or Li in China, for all she knew. She definitely needed more solid details before going to the authorities.

"We are happy to help agents of CITES," Kuang said in good English. "I am pleased to say that in recent years we have cracked down on the trade in products from endangered species. For one example, since we outlawed finning, the sale of shark fin soup has dropped by almost eighty-five percent."

"I know. That's good news, I believe," Gene said approvingly. "I realize that the task you have is immense and I appreciate your co-operation, sir." Gene shook Kuang's hand. "If I have any details to pass to you?"

"Please take my card and telephone me direct." Mr.

Kuang proffered his card with both hands, fingertips only touching it, and bowed slightly.

"And here is mine." Gene copied the polite gesture with his business card.

"Good hunting, sir."

Gene gave a slight bow. "Thank you, Mr. Kuang."

They left the office.

Once outside, Gene read the card Mr. Kuang had given him then handed it to her. "You keep it."

"I'll add it to my collection. Gene..."

"Yes, dear?"

"What's 'finning'?"

"Ah, yes. They catch the shark, cut off its fins and toss the poor thing into the sea to die."

She shuddered. "That's awful...so callous!"

"I know, my love." He gestured vaguely at the boats berthed at the jetty. "Any particular yacht caught your fancy?"

"No, I don't see myself as a sailor, thanks." She hesitated, and then plunged in, "I did see something of interest, though. It may be nothing...but..."

"What was that?"

"I think I saw details of a boat belonging to that oligarch the Spanish are looking for, Belofsky."

He stopped walking, turned to face her. "Where?"

"The boat is called the *Izolda*. It's berthed here."

Gene pursed his lips in thought. "Are you sure it's him?"

"No, otherwise I'd have mentioned it in there."

He checked his watch. "Blast, I'm cutting it fine as it is. I've got to be in the city center in twenty minutes."

"Seeing Daphne again?"

"Yes."

"She's a brave lady."

"She is. Look, I think this *Izolda* thing can wait."

"I'm sure it can." She pointed to a poster on a wall, advertising the forthcoming Oil Symposium in the city tomorrow night. "I'd bet if it is Belofsky he's attending that."

"Interesting... Sara, love, can you...?"

"Of course. I'll make my own way back to the hotel. Okay?"

"Yes, thanks, dear. Be careful—and no snooping around any yachts with the name of *Izolda* or anything else. When I've got a moment, I'll get in touch with Lieutenant Vargas in Tenerife."

"Right." They kissed briefly and he hurried away.

Sara pivoted on her heel and studied the waterfront. To her left was a container ship, berthed at the jetty, a huge crane hovering. That section of the dockside was separated by a high fence. To her right were five luxury cruisers. The *Izolda* shouldn't be too hard to locate, she reckoned.

No snooping, Gene said. Well, she didn't agree to that, did she?

Wuxi-Nanjing

Cat, Yubi, Rick and Bing caught the slightly faster G-train at Wuxi station for Nanjing. It was packed. The train sped through the outskirts dominated by huge residential tower blocks and skyscrapers, a handful still under construction. Rick had joked, "China might be great, when they finish it."

Despite the constant almost deafening chatter, they managed to make each other heard.

"We need to go to Nanjing because I've heard worrying news from my cousin Linghao," Bing explained.

"Another cousin?" Rick queried, amused.

"We have big families. The 'planned birth' social engineering of a one-child policy had many exemptions and in fact was only designed for a single generation."

"What about fines for having more than one child?" Rick asked.

"Many parents believe that two are better than one," Yubi said. "The fines are organized by each province, and the exemptions are numerous and varied. And there are no penalties for twins or multiple births."

"So there must be a queue at fertility clinics?" Cat suggested.

Bing chuckled. "Yes, the number of twins born in the last few years does seem to have doubled."

"I hope you don't mind me asking," Rick said, "but what about the imbalance between the number of boys and girls?"

"Yes, that is sad," Bing said. "Boys are prized above girls and yes, some girl babies are given away or abandoned."

"That's dreadful!" Cat said.

"I agree," Bing said. "*Boys are like gold*, they say. *Girls are like water in a basin; after a while you pour it out*. Thousands are still abandoned, despite a parent being jailed for up to five years for discarding an infant. There are official baby refuges and they seem to encourage parents to abandon their babies. And don't get me on the black market of baby traffickers!"

Cat shook her head and then said firmly, "So, to get back to your cousin."

Rick grinned. "Was she this single-minded at university?"

Bing smirked. "Yes. That's why she got good grades."

"Linghao, your cousin?" Cat prompted.

"Ah, Linghao. He works in the Ananke factory in Nanjing. They produce longevity drugs, goji berry pills, destined for Japan, Hong Kong, Macao, and Taiwan."

"Well, this is more like the Ananke I know," Cat said. "I still can't get my head round them manufacturing lucky cats!"

Rick nudged her gently with an elbow. "On track?"

She pulled a face at him. "Of course. Go on, then."

"Did you say Japan?" Rick asked Bing. "Haven't they already got plenty of people aged over one hundred. Isn't there a woman aged 117?"

"Yes," Cat added, "as I recall, she said she owes her long life to sushi!"

"Maybe that is so," Bing said. "Sushi or not, there's a market in Japan for goji berries. The main exporter does well out of it, but Ananke has found a niche, even beginning to outsell the Chinese firm—they're combining the goji berries with raw fish, all in a health-care supplement pill."

"Is it approved?" Cat asked.

"Oh, yes. Approved by the Ministry of Public Health. Approval for healthcare products is easier than getting the nod for food products."

"What is the worrying news your cousin has?" Cat asked.

"I don't know. You need to talk to Linghao. I think it

has something to do with the Japanese market, though. He says there's a lot of anti-Japanese feeling here at present. It might have to do with those uninhabited islets Diaoyu..."

Rick looked blank.

"They're disputed islands in the East China Sea," Yubi explained.

"There's a lot of publicity concerning the fly-by activities of the Russian warplanes close to the UK," Cat added. "If a mistake is made, the consequences could be dire. And now we have China dispatching its warplanes in similar fashion—and risking conflict with Japan by default."

Bing agreed. "I've written about this. Several Japanese islands in the East China Sea are in dispute with our government. The Japanese air base at Naha scrambled more than four hundred times last year. These fly-bys also imperil ties between our two nations."

Yubi released a heavy sigh. "It's like another arms race."

Bing turned to Cat. "Both countries claim ownership of the uninhabited islets—known as Senkaku in Japan and Diaoyu here in China—presently administered by Japan. This dispute affects Japanese investment here in China, which can't be good."

"The tensions with Taiwan are dire, too," Yubi added. "Our air-force keeps nudging, provoking..."

Cat added, "I read earlier this year President Xi Jinping said that Taiwan would face the 'punishment of history' for any attempts at separatism. To me, that comes across as a direct threat."

"You're right," Bing said. "Xi has strong words

regarding Taiwan. He does not exclude force as a means to unifying Taiwan with the mainland."

"Unifying or destroying?" Yubi said solemnly.

Rick shuddered.

Cat whispered somberly, "What with the saber-rattling here about Taiwan, the pressures from Putin in the Ukraine, the never-ending mess in North Africa and the Middle East, and the murdering ISIL jihadists, the world now seems a very dangerous place."

Nanjing

Song entered the reception foyer of the office block. It seemed strange, returning in a different role. He was surprised to see Jia, his middle-aged bespectacled secretary at the reception desk.

Jia bowed briefly; her flashing eyes showed she was clearly pleased to see him. "Welcome, sir."

He bowed in response. "I have missed your cheery smile, Jia. Have you had a job change, then?"

"No, sir. Meilin is sick and I volunteered to take her place here. Mr. Heng doesn't need me today."

"Is Mr. Heng in?"

"I don't know, sir, I only came on an hour ago. I'll check." She scanned the book on her desk, slid a finger over the columns, and then peered at him through the top half of her bifocals. "No. He hasn't come in yet."

He studied the wall clock behind her desk: 11:00. It was unlike Heng. He was a dedicated company man. "Can I wait for him in...his office?"

"Yes, of course, Mr. Song. Would you like me to arrange for coffee to be sent to you?"

"That would be most appreciated. Thank you, Jia." He bowed and made his way to his old office on the second floor.

He opened the door. The office was a little tidier than he was used to, so that was something else in Heng's favor. His replacement had also moved the furniture around, doubtless to appease his feng shui gods.

Song sat at the desk and leafed through Heng's diary.

Yesterday, a scribbled note to visit Wuxi. And then it was clear. No appointments for today.

He eased back in the chair, swung it from side to side, pondering. What aroused Heng's interest in Wuxi? That "special shipment"?

A rapid knock sounded on the door, made him jump.

It was unlike Jia to knock and wait. She usually knocked and walked straight in. Then he berated himself. Jia would be on reception now. She must have arranged for someone else to bring the coffee.

"Come in!" he called.

Jia entered, consternation on her face. She carried a silver tray that held his mug of coffee and a plate with four shortbread biscuits, his favorites. "Sir, I'm sorry, so sorry..." She lowered the tray to the desk, and then peeped over her shoulder.

Two policemen in uniform now stood in the doorway. Not a courtesy call, but official business, since they still wore their hats.

Jia gestured at them. "Mr. Song, this is Inspector Hou and Sergeant Yu. They have bad news for you."

"Thank you, Jia."

She bobbed her head at him, trailed a shaky hand across her eyes and left.

Song stood up, beckoned. "Come in, Inspector, Sergeant."

Hou was an inspector third class, judging by his shoulder insignia: one pip and two bars. He was thin, his face long and drawn, the dark eyes brightly shining from sunken sockets. Perhaps in his early forties; his countenance held a world weariness about it.

Yu was a sergeant second class: two pips and one bar. He was shorter than his superior, squat, and his jacket was too taut, stretching across his belly; his eyes were close together and seemed to permanently squint. He appeared to be slightly younger than the inspector, but not much. Song suspected that Yu fed his stomach because he no longer hungered for further promotion.

"What bad news do you have for me?"

The two policemen entered the office and halted at the desk, facing him, removed their hats and slid them under their arms. The sergeant held a notebook and pencil awkwardly, squashing his hat with the pressure of his arm.

The inspector said, "I regret to inform you that your fellow employee Mr. Heng has been found dead at his home."

Song frowned. "I must assume that his death was not from natural causes?"

"That is astute of you, sir," said Hou.

Shrugging off the compliment, Song said, "Well,

since it appears to be a police matter, can you tell me how he died?"

Hou's gaze was level, unblinking; not quite inscrutable, but close. "It will be no secret before too long. Mr. Heng was shot. Murdered."

Song let out an involuntary gasp. He hadn't expected that! "Shot?" He noticed that Sergeant Yu was scribbling in his notebook; doubtless recording physical as well as verbal responses.

"Yes, sir," Hou replied. "His neighbors said there was a commotion in his apartment—it is on the ground floor—and then they distinctly heard a shot. A man was seen running away."

"This is most distressing. Did the neighbors provide you with a description of the fleeing man?"

Hou shook his head. "Their description fits the majority of men, sir, and is of little help."

"Help... So, how can I assist you, Inspector?"

"Do you possess any knowledge regarding Mr. Heng's private life? Was he liable to gamble or get involved in any dubious enterprise or associate with undesirables?"

President Xi had expressed a strong desire to clamp down on corruption. Clearly, this injunction colored any investigation.

Song lifted his shoulders in apology. "I'm sorry, I can't think of anything, or anyone." He did wonder about Heng's concern regarding the "special shipment" at Wuxi. But that was too tenuous to contemplate or voice. "From the tenor of your questions, you don't seem to think it was an intruder."

"No, I don't. Nothing was disturbed. The door was not forced. Whoever the man was, Mr. Heng knew him. That is why I am given pause to wonder about his private life. If he had become involved with unsavory people, for example."

"Mr. Heng was a fine employee, a man of good integrity and that is why he was selected for this post. In fact, he had only recently relieved me at this job."

"That is most interesting, sir," the inspector said with the hint of a smile. "So, why are you here now, in the murdered man's office?"

Chapter 13

Evil Lurked

Shanghai

As soon as Gene arrived in Daphne's office, he could tell she was excited. "What's the news?" he asked.

"It's all good," she said. She told him that the police had made the arrests and the case would be pursued.

"Must be ready for a celebratory drink, eh?" he asked, guiltily thinking of Sara. She knew he had to work, but having a drink with a fellow agent didn't really constitute work.

"No." Daphne raised a hand. "We have more business to transact."

"Oh?"

"I arranged this yesterday." She went to the wall safe, whirled the combination wheel, opened the door and took out a wad of dollar bills. "You'll need this."

"What for?"

"I've arranged for you to meet a dealer. I've told him you're interested in buying a tiger skin."

"What's my reason?"

"It's for your girlfriend."

"Will they believe that?"

"That's what I told him. You're rich and eager to please the woman of your dreams."

"Woman of nightmares, more like, if she wants a poor dead animal's skin." He put the money away.

"As you say. Still, if you offer enough money, he will believe you." She patted his jacket, where the chest now bulged. "Settle on that $20,000. Not a cent more."

Wuxi-Nanjing

As the train sped along at a fair lick, Bing said, "Most goji berries are grown in the Ningxia Hui region—that's Northern China. They eat them daily. In fact, reports say that there are about sixteen times as many people who are a hundred years old or older there as in the rest of the country."

"Sounds convincing," Rick said. "But I've got a natural disinclination to believe statistics. I call it my 'climate change syndrome'."

"As a journalist, I think a bit of skepticism is healthy," Bing said. "Naturally, I have to be careful regarding government statistics... Even so, elderly residents of the Ningxia Hui region do seem much more active and healthy than their peers in Western cultures. The berries are referred to as 'the longevity fruit'. The west is only now waking up to its properties. If it takes off in Japan in a big way, it will spread to the US and then Europe. It could be a big money-spinner."

"Which explains Dante's interest," Cat said.

"Yes, Dante likes money," Rick added.

The train took a little over an hour to arrive at Nanjing.

Shanghai

Sara Whitney stood in the shadow of a yacht on the dock; it rested on huge trestles, doubtless undergoing repair, perhaps having its bottom scraped, or whatever they called it. From here she had an uninterrupted view of the cruiser *Izolda,* which was berthed stern facing the jetty. It was a big boat, and sleek looking—three decks above the waterline, all seeming to thrust forward; streamlining, she supposed.

She watched for a good fifteen minutes, but there was no sign of anybody on the cruiser. The short gangplank—or was it gangway?—was enticing; the far end fitted into the fifth countersunk step, which led onto what was doubtless the main deck. She fidgeted with the strap of her shoulder bag.

It wouldn't do any harm to get a closer look. If only to prove that the owner was the same Belofsky the Spanish Guardia Civil sought.

She slipped out of the shadow and approached the dockside. A casual glance to left and right confirmed that nobody was about; the four boats on either side of the *Izolda* bobbed slightly with the slight swell from the river traffic. She was aware her Punt Roma dress and high heels were not appropriate for any vessel, but since there was no one to observe, it didn't matter. It wasn't as if she was going sailing into the blue yonder.

Gingerly, she trod onto the gangway that sloped upwards, her shoes making a faint clacking sound. She stopped, gripped the solid metal rail for support and removed her shoes; she'd carry them, it made for a quieter approach. Tread carefully, she told herself: there were horizontal protrusions, probably designed to prevent people slipping, though she feared she'd stub her toes on the damned things. Still, after about seven paces, she'd reached the end of the gangway and climbed onto the next wood-covered step. Two more steps and finally she lowered her feet onto the deck, which moved a little as the boat bobbed, but she'd coped with worse motion on ferries.

As she sat on a couch and put on her shoes, she warily scanned around.

She was trespassing. If she was accosted, she needed a plausible story. Lost didn't quite cut it, did it? Looking for a friend on his yacht the *Isobel*? That might work. Of course, she assumed that anyone she faced would speak English—or, perhaps French or Spanish. That was her limit with languages.

On the left and right were stairs that spiraled up to the next deck. In front of her were sliding glass doors. She moved to these and peered through. She let out a gasp and blinked. It didn't seem possible, but she was looking at a bar lounge, a long and broad dining room, with a table and six chairs, all stylishly furnished, and beyond, a door that led heaven knows where. It reminded her of Dr. Who's time-traveling Tardis, bigger inside than appearances suggested from the outside.

That area was bigger than her first apartment, she reckoned with a hint of jealousy.

Nobody about—no crew or owners. She tried the door. It was locked.

Relief flowed through her. That was a sign. Maybe she should go, get off now.

Her mouth was dry and she sensed her heartbeat had increased. Nerves or adrenaline made her jumpy. It was a silly idea, anyway. And it was totally counter to Gene's admonition.

She glanced at the stairs to her right, wondering where they led. Despite her misgivings, she was intrigued to see how the other half lived. She had no idea how much this yacht cost, but it must be in the hundreds of thousands—pounds, euros or even dollars, it didn't much matter, it was beyond her rather mundane dreams.

Before she knew it, she was climbing the stairs.

She emerged on another deck, this one generously filled with seats and a low table; on her left, more glass doors, but these were opaque. From this elevated position, she could see more of the river.

Emboldened, she looked at the next set of stairs. Might as well climb them. Get an even better view.

At the top, she stepped onto a wooden deck. In front of her were more seats and a Jacuzzi. Nobody here, either. All this luxury, yet unused, idly standing by for the whim of the filthy rich. She eyed the Jacuzzi: well, maybe not filthy.

Time to get off this boat. She wasn't going to discover anything. It had been a foolish idea. She didn't intend telling Gene about this little escapade. He'd simply blow his top. And his reaction would be justified.

She turned to descend the stairs and her stomach abruptly seemed to twist and squirm. Her heart sank and she swallowed.

"This *is* an unexpected surprise," said Alita Lopez, grinning. Alita levelled an automatic pistol at her. She wore a skimpy yellow bikini; the operation scar from her midriff wound showed white against the tan.

Sara froze, unable to respond.

"Staying silent is a good idea," Alita murmured. "If you said something to upset me, I might shoot you—and believe me, this Beretta holds thirteen nine-millimeter rounds which would make a mess of your pretty dress."

Despite the woman's words, Sara still feared Alita was going to shoot. Her skin went cold, and her heart pounded. *Oh, Gene, what have I done?*

———

DAPHNE AND GENE walked along a back street. Apartment blocks stood shoulder to shoulder, column upon column of air-conditioning units seeming to replace windows and even external walls. All of those units working overtime in today's oppressive heat. All of them burning energy; so much for eco-consciousness.

Several shop-fronts were closed, the majority of them boarded up. Squeezed between two empty shops was a small emporium, its window filled with leather and fur jackets. "Is this it?" he asked.

Daphne nodded. "They don't put their wares in the window, you know." She reached into her shoulder bag and switched on her camera. "Ready, time to act the love-sick rich boy."

He opened the door. The bell above the jamb tinkled.

It was dark inside.

Immediately in front of them were racks of leather jackets. The smell of leather was pervasive. Beyond the racks was a long counter and behind it a bead curtain. On the walls to the left and right hung animal skins— zebra, lion and tiger. Gene sensed his stomach overturn and feared he was going to be sick. He'd seen tusks and even the feet of elephants, and rhino horn, not to mention the intricate scrimshaw work of ivory carvers; all that had been upsetting. Yet seeing the animals' whole skin felt that much worse; horrendous. Evil lurked in here, he believed; not merely death, but something else, a soulless vile presence permeated the very air.

Abruptly, a Chinese man emerged through the bead curtain, hardly making a sound as he moved to the counter. "Can I help you?" He was thin, angular and wore a pigtail.

"We spoke yesterday," Daphne said, gesturing at Gene. "My boss wants to see a Siberian tiger skin. You said you could get hold of one undamaged."

"I remember." The man half-turned, called into the back, "Mei, bring the tiger we received this morning."

In response, a petite woman carried the skin draped over her shoulder, most of it trailing behind. She moved with a shuffling gait and dropped her load onto the counter.

The man smoothed it out, at least six feet in length. "Beautiful, is it not?" he said.

Daphne stepped forward, strategically placed her shoulder bag to one side and examined the skin. "It is good." She shoved a finger in a hole in the throat area. "One clean shot."

"Our harvesters are crack shots."

"I can see," Gene said.

The shopkeeper glared at him and said impatiently, "Well?"

Gene stroked the fur, and immediately felt unclean. "I'll offer you $15,000."

The man's face clouded and his eyes narrowed. He glared at Daphne. "You said he was serious!"

Gene tapped the skin. "Look here, I have to get it through customs—that will cost me."

"That is your problem," the man snapped. "$25,000. Take it or leave it. There will be other buyers."

"My girl really wants one exactly like this..." He fished in his jacket inside pocket and pulled out a wad of high denomination dollar bills, flicked them. "I can go to $20,000."

"Make it $22,000 and it is yours."

"I would like to," Gene said, "but as you can see, this is all I have on me. I could go to the bank, get the rest..."

The man's eyes darted from the dollar bills to Gene's face, then to Daphne and the skin. "No, I will settle." Without fail, an immediate cash sale was always too tempting. "You drive a hard bargain."

Gene grinned. "My girlfriend doesn't think so, I can tell you!" He handed the man the wad of cash.

"Wrap it up," the man told Mei. Then he began licking his finger and counting the dollar bills.

"Do I get a bill of sale?" Gene asked.

"No. You can see the quality of the merchandise." The man shoved the money in his trouser pocket. "I hope your girlfriend likes it." He turned on his heel and passed through the bead curtain, leaving Mei to tie the brown paper package with string.

When she had finished, Mei shoved it across the counter, gave a fleeting smile and a brief bow and made a shuffling retreat into the rear of the shop, too.

The package was heavy. He marveled that Mei had been able to carry it so effortlessly. "Let's go," he said.

The door-bell tinkled, announcing their departure.

Outside, Gene shuddered and felt grubby.

As they walked away, he said, "How do you do this job, Daphne?"

"I'm fortunate to get the chance to actively work against these people for the good of the natural world. I think of the good, rather than the bad."

"Now, it's back to the office and then we get in touch with the police, right?"

"Yes. Show them the videos. I will make copies as well."

"And they'll arrest that man and confiscate the money?"

"Yes."

When they finally reached the car, Daphne said, "You'd better put that thing in the trunk. I hope you have your ID from CITES in case we're stopped and searched." She pointed to the ubiquitous CCTV street cameras.

"Wouldn't go anywhere without it!" He dropped the weighty package in the trunk, slammed it shut and slid in the passenger seat next to Daphne.

As she drove away from the curb, he asked, "How long will the process take now?"

"The police are primed already. As soon as I have made digital copies of the videos, we can show them. They will get authorization for a raid."

"Couldn't they have done that while we were there?"

"I don't want my cover blown. If I was there at the time of arrests, it would look suspicious if I wasn't charged as well."

"I'd better phone my partner, tell her it could be a while yet. She may have to settle on a KFC at this rate!" He opened his phone and rang Sara.

She didn't pick up. Probably having a shower. He could sympathize, as Shanghai weather sapped the strength, even at this time of year. And, besides, he felt unclean having touched that poor animal's skin.

SARA'S CELL-PHONE RANG. Automatically, her hand went to her handbag.

"Don't answer it!" Alita snapped, her eyes lancing at her. "Drop your bag to the deck—slowly!"

Sara unslung the bag, lowered it to the wooden deck.

"Now, move away from the top of the stairs."

Obediently, Sara backed a couple of paces. It was illegal to carry a firearm in China, she knew, but that wouldn't bother Alita. Illegal was probably her middle name. *She wouldn't shoot me here, surely? It was too public!* Then again, she hadn't seen a soul about on the dockside. And Alita's trigger finger must be itching to get her revenge.

As if reading her thoughts, Alita said, "I'd like to shoot you where you stand, but I can think of more amusing things to do with you." Keeping her gun trained and steady, she moved a couple of paces forward, picked up Sara's bag, opened it and emptied the contents on the deck. She fleetingly peered at the cell-phone: it flashed *Missed call: Gene.* "So, your partner wants to get in touch, does he?"

Tears welled but Sara blinked them away. Keep her talking. Maybe somebody would arrive on the jetty, become an awkward witness. "Where do you keep your gun—I don't see anywhere suitable in that skimpy outfit."

Alita raised an eyebrow and posed. "Like it? Designer label, of course..."

Sara made no comment, merely glared.

"If you must know," Alita snapped, "I was going to cool off in the Jacuzzi. I happened to look over the side and saw you sneak aboard. So I slipped below, went inside and got my gun. I followed you here. You always were too nosy."

Keeping the gun levelled on Sara, Alita replaced the contents of the bag, slung its strap on her own shoulder. Then she waggled the Beretta. "Right, go slowly; use the other stairs. Don't try anything stupid. I won't hesitate to shoot!"

Sara gazed around, but there was nobody within shouting distance, and even if there had been, she didn't know what *help* was in Mandarin.

The bitch must have read her mind—again. "The word you're searching for is *jiùmìng!*"

Chapter 14

Lions' Heads

Nanjing

Cat, Yubi, Rick and Bing left the railway station and walked the short distance to the Shuguang International Hotel. "Yes, I'm paying," Cat said. "And I brook no argument."

They registered. Cat found the staff to be polite and helpful and allocated a single room for Yubi, while Rick and Cat had a double, and Bing would share with Linghao when he arrived.

Shortly after they'd freshened up, they all met at the hotel's restaurant, which was on the thirty-second floor.

Bing explained that he had phoned Linghao from their room. "He will join us after dinner."

The food was good—steamed belly pork with ground rice for some, and pork meatballs braised with Chinese leaf, resembling lions' heads, for others—while the view over the city was marvelous.

As promised, Linghao was shown to their table

149

shortly after dessert. He wore a dark gray suit that was at least a size too small for his corpulent frame. He had round cheeks, small close-set eyes, protruding ears, and a snub nose.

Bing welcomed him and made introductions, speaking in English, adding, "You're sharing a room with me, cousin."

"Oh, the last time we shared, you snored and kept me awake all night!"

"I'll try not to tonight," Bing promised, pouring Shaoxing rice wine for Linghao, which was still warm.

They made a toast: "*Ganbei!*" Bottoms up.

Settling into his chair, Linghao eyed Cat and said, "Bing told me of your interest in Ananke."

"I'd like to thank you for seeing us," she said. "And compliment you on your English."

His chest visibly swelled. "It was Bing's influence. He twisted my arm to take night-classes. Now, I have reasonable English, after four years..."

"Well, it was time well spent. So, what concerns you about the factory here, Linghao?"

He sipped the wine. "It started innocently enough. I joined a local history group and I recognized a couple of fellow workers who were already attending. After a few sessions, though, I realized that all they were interested in was 1937. They kept harping on about it. I began to fear it was too morbid."

"What was special about that date?" Rick said.

"The second Sino-Japanese war," Yubi explained.

"More precisely, the massacre of Nanjing," Cat supplied.

"Massacre... Some call it rape," Bing interjected. "Even now, many refer to it as the forgotten holocaust."

Linghao said, "It is a sore that has festered all these years between our two countries. I can't understand it. The two fellow workers seemed to take it personally, yet they weren't there or even born when it happened; it was too long ago. Anyway, they became so intense about it that I decided to leave the group."

"You're right, Linghao. Dwelling on an eighty-year-old horrific past isn't healthy," Cat said in sympathy. "Besides, if anyone survived, they must have been children or infants; the adults of that time would be long dead."

"Unless they ate goji berries and lived longer?" Rick added.

"Sometimes you can be too flippant, Rick," Cat chided.

"Sorry. I was trying to lighten the mood."

Cat patted his knee. "I know." She turned to Bing. "Of course not all the Japanese were so evil, you know."

"Says who?" snapped Linghao.

"Cathy will tell you, if you're patient, cousin," Bing said. "She may not know about our tensions, but she's studied Europe's."

Cat smiled at Bing. "It was 1940. The Nazis had been hounding Jews for years. In Poland, the Japanese Consul Sempo Sugihara was aware of the fate that awaited those who didn't get away. So before his expulsion from the city, he issued over three thousand visas for Jews to travel east, through Moscow and Siberia to Japan and beyond. There's no telling how many he saved from being 'selected' for the death camps."

"I didn't know that," Linghao said, mollified.

"Me neither," Rick said.

Cat leaned forward, and said, her tone somber,

"But, Linghao, where is this leading? What have your two intense fellow workers got to do with anything?"

"I'd overheard those two whispering. They work late a lot and seem to be planning something."

"But what?" Cat demanded. "Sabotage the plant?"

"Doing your job for you, Cathy," Rick suggested with the hint of a smile.

She gave him a firm stare and didn't smile. "We've been through this—I wouldn't repeat the mistake I made at Anger. I don't want to lose people their jobs. I just want to harm Dante and his company."

"There's the rub," Rick said. "Harm his company and the employees will suffer eventually when they go out of business."

Yubi spoke up: "But why would they sabotage a foreign firm's plant that has nothing to do with Japan—apart from sales, that is?"

"Perhaps we could find out," Linghao said. "They both go to a bar most nights after work."

"Fancy a drink?" Bing asked, emptying his glass, a twinkle in his eye.

Shanghai

There was a disconcerting twinkle in Alita's eyes as she said, "When we're at sea, I'll enjoy making you pay."

Sara didn't respond, but continued to descend the stairs.

When she reached the main deck again, Alita said, "Through there." She opened the glass doors, passed the bar and lounge area, then the dining table adequate for eight place settings. "Open the door slowly."

The doorway led into a huge space, more like an apartment than a bedroom, with a bathroom on the left, a double bed, and a flat screen television. Sara hesitated and received a push in the small of her back. "This is our cabin—mine and Anton's. Yours is not far." She indicated another door. Open it."

This led into a compact cabin area with a computer, printer, a bureau, and two seats, a table, and a bookshelf. On the other side of the office was yet another door. "That is your room," Alita said. "Go on."

Sara entered a cabin which was much smaller than the last bedroom. Directly opposite the door was a double bed; on the right, a wash-basin and closet; on the left, a shower cubicle and a dressing table.

"Here we are," Alita said. "Get used to your new home." Absently, her free hand rubbed the operation scar that showed white against her natural tan. She waved the Beretta. "Lie on the bed, face up."

Obediently, Sara sat on the bed, shucked off her shoes and lay down. Her heart pounded and her stomach quivered, perhaps in fear. What was Alita Lopez planning? She anticipated hurt, pain, but clung to Lopez's words—she wasn't going to make her pay until they were at sea. Why lie here, though? Her mouth was dry; still, she had no intention of asking any questions.

"Good." Alita dropped Sara's handbag on the dressing table and moved to the side of the bed—on Sara's right, where she sat on the edge, her hip brushing against Sara's bare arm. Sara flinched at the contact. "Lift your arm to the bedhead."

Sara hesitated, fearful.

"Do it!" Alita raised her gun, threateningly.

Sara raised her arm.

Alarmingly fast, Alita's hand darted and released a switch on the bedhead. A handcuff popped out of a niche and Alita clicked it firmly round Sara 's right wrist.

Instinctively, Sara tugged at it, but it held firm and she only succeeded in hurting her wrist.

"Be still, you foolish woman."

"Isn't this a little bit kinky?" Sara managed to say, her voice a croak, her throat so parched.

"It depends on the social circles you move in, I suppose. You are completely within my power, so behave and I will try to be nice."

Nice? Sara bit on a retort and turned her head, looked at the window or porthole or whatever it was called. It was square, like a window, though. Absently, she felt her left wrist and then her ankles being shackled to the bed frame. The pit of her stomach squirmed; queasy, unsettled.

She returned her gaze to Alita, who removed Sara's wristwatch and then moved to the dressing table.

Alita had put the gun next to the handbag and the watch lay beside it. Sara realized she now had no way of telling the passage of time. Alita then extracted Sara's cell-phone from the bag and placed it there as well. She extracted a notepad which was folded open at a page with their hotel written in Chinese characters which Sara had use to give directions to taxi drivers; it saved her trying to mangle Mandarin. Alita sniggered at this and ripped out the page, said, "You won't need this. You won't be seeing your hotel again, ever." She crumpled the sheet into a little ball and tossed it on the floor and then removed a small card and tore it up. Sara remembered: it held the contact details for the harbor official, Kuang; Gene had given it to her an hour or so ago, if that.

Gene! She stared at the phone; it remained silent.

Tears pricked her eyes and soon blurred her vision, covered her cheeks.

"Never mind," Alita said, "I'm sure your brave partner will come to rescue you soon!" She smirked and left the cabin, slamming the door behind her.

Alone, incapable of getting free, Sara had a sour taste in her mouth and her restricted limbs quivered. A weight pressed on her chest, her heartbeat heavy. Dark presentiment hovered, and she found it difficult to breathe. Maybe these effects were because she was hungry? Gene was supposed to be taking her for a meal tonight. Her stomach rumbled and roiled. Easy, she told herself. Steady, now. Her breathing was soon in control. She eyed the cell-phone again and fought down a sob. This was no time for self-pity.

Chapter 15

"Such delicious innocence."

Nanjing

It was dark when they all left the hotel and strolled along the riverfront. "This is the Qinhuai River," Bing told Rick. "It stretches over one hundred kilometers. The cradle of age-old Nanjing civilization."

"Oh? Cradle, in what way?"

"Since ancient times," Bing explained, "it has been the tributary of the Yangtze. It is referred to as the 'life blood of Nanjing'...though, in truth, much Chinese blood has flowed in the river..."

"Past atrocities, committed by rulers?" Rick suggested. Too late he detected Cathy's admonishing look.

"No, Rick, far from it," Bing said, staring out to the river. "On the banks of the Yangtze on December 18, 1937, one of those days of infamy, Japanese soldiers took most of the morning tying the hands together of all of the captured Chinese soldiers or civilians. The prisoners were divided into four columns, and machine-gunned where they stood."

"That's horrendous!" Rick exclaimed. "A war crime?"

"Yes. Unable to escape, the prisoners could only scream and thrash about in desperation."

Rick levelled his gaze on Cathy. "You knew about this?"

"Sadly, yes. The rape of Nanjing is one of those slices of history I'd rather not have known." She tapped her temple. "Once the details are imbedded there, you can't erase them from your memory. Ever." Her eyes glistened in the light from the river.

"It's certainly colorful," Rick said, pointing to the lantern-decorated boats, their lights contrasting with the starlit sky and glistening reflecting water.

Rick's deliberate changing of the subject seemed to work, and the solemn pall dissipated as a tourist cruise boat passed by. Linghao pointed to it. "If you had the time to spare, you could enjoy a cruise. There are many attractions: the Zhanyuan Garden, Confucius Temple, Egret Islet, and China Gate."

"And," added Bing, "all the sailing boats on the river, the pavilions and towers on the riverbanks. It is a perfect tourist sight, where gardens, barges, streets and folk culture and customs blend."

"You haven't changed, Bing!" Cat said with a laugh. "You're talking like a tour guide..."

"...or a journalist?" he offered

She laughed again. "I suppose you've written articles about the river?"

"I have. Apart from sightseeing, the riverside is also a popular place to taste the local cuisine."

"I think we've eaten enough for tonight," Yubi said.

"What a pity. No room for the specialties like steamed buns stuffed with pork, eight-flavored jellied bean curd pastries, roasted beef, and salted duck?"

"Bing, stop!" Cat exclaimed. "Or I'll burst simply thinking about it!"

Linghao tittered. "Now you've walked off that food, I'll take you in my minivan to the bar I told you about."

Shanghai

Gene let himself into their hotel room and called out, "Sara, I'm back!" He shut the door. "Sorry I kept you waiting!" He'd have a quick shower and change and then they could go down to the restaurant before the place closed.

The lack of any answer was odd.

He crossed the spacious bedroom, noting that it appeared just as they'd left it earlier today, only tidier, since the staff had clearly been in to clean the room and make the bed.

By the time he reached the en suite bathroom, he sensed anxiety stabbing at his gut. Go away, there has to be a rational explanation. She wasn't here. And the shower cubicle was completely dry, fresh towels provided. He checked the closet and decided she mustn't have returned from the dockside, since the dress she'd worn then wasn't hanging up.

His flesh went cold. He'd last seen her at the dock-side. Visions of her falling off the jetty intruded. No, don't be stupid, she can swim very well. Then why hadn't she answered her phone or rung him?

Sara, where the hell are you?

He pulled out his phone and speed-dialed her number.

————————

Nanjing

As Ying, the factory chief, left his office and got into his car, he mulled over the phone call he had received earlier.

The speaker hadn't identified himself, but he had been assertive and gave the impression that he knew things that were very secret. That was worrying. The man was as bothersome as Heng, but he gave the impression of being more careful. Until now. It would be doubly difficult, however, to remove this threat because there were two of them, or so the speaker had implied.

Ying was not looking forward to the meeting in the dive they had nominated. He knew that his red velveteen jacket with Mandarin collar and white shirt were not appropriate for the place, but he would not lower his dress standards for them or anyone. He believed it gave him a measure of superiority. He felt confident, not least because his QSZ-92 5.8mm automatic pistol pressed snugly against his chest.

He parked two blocks away. He had employed similar tactics when paying Heng that fatal visit.

Locking the car, he removed a cigar from his pocket and lit it.

A leisurely stroll to the *Mòlí Huà* bar.

Shanghai

Sara's phone trilled, its light coming on, and it vibrated, shuddering on the dressing table. She guessed it was Gene trying to contact her. She cried tears of frustration and tugged in vain at the metal cuffs.

The bedroom door opened and Alita strode in. Behind Alita stood Belofsky, his eyes dancing at sight of her.

Sara cringed. She looked at her phone as it persisted to ring.

Picking up the phone, Alita said, "Anton, should I answer it? It's her partner calling. I can assure him that she's unharmed. I could bring him to us."

"No," Belofsky said. "We'd have no guarantee that he would come alone. He might tell someone where he was going, too." He smiled coldly. "Let it ring."

"As you wish." Alita put it on the dressing table, and then turned back to Belofsky. "But won't its signal reveal where she is?"

Shaking his head, Belofsky leaned against the door frame and folded his arms, studying Sara with lascivious eyes. "He won't have that kind of clout here, my dear. He's a CITES man, interested in illegal trade in endangered species. They're not going to organize a trace for him, simply because he's mislaid his partner!" He snickered. "So, Miss Sara Whitney, Alita tells me you decided to pay us a visit."

Sara pursed her lips and glared at him.

"As I told you, she was snooping around," Alita said, scowling.

Belofsky indicated Sara's phone. "It would be gratifying to have her partner here cuffed as well, I must admit. But I cannot postpone our arrangements. If Brin should fall into our hands, it will be most unfortunate in his case. If not, well, it will still be unfortunate for him, no?"

"What do you mean?" Sara asked, a quaver in her voice.

"He either dies or he loses his partner," Alita explained, shrugging. "One or the other."

Tears welled in Sara's eyes and her heart sank. "What are you going to do with me?"

"Don't worry," Alita said. "We'll take good care of you. Anton looks after his merchandise."

"Merchandise?"

"Sometimes, my dear," Belofsky said with a snicker, "I wonder how you caused us so much trouble, I really do. Such delicious innocence, even from a sexually active woman."

Sara's cheeks flushed hotly.

Alita added, "What Anton means is, you will be sold."

Sara shivered as a chill invaded her nerves. "White slave trade," she groaned, "is that it?"

Alita wagged a finger at her. "That's a racist remark, Miss Whitney. You should be more careful what you say—and who you say it to."

Belofsky sat on the bedside and studied Sara.

Sara shifted her gaze to the porthole.

He touched her ankle and she flinched, involuntarily tried to pull her leg away, but couldn't.

Slowly, he eased his hand along her shin and lifted the hem of her dress above her knee, gently squeezing her flesh.

His warm touch made her squirm inside.

"I wonder if she is really a blonde." He turned to Alita, his eyes earnest. "I would really like to know."

Alita sashayed forward, playfully slapped his hand away. "Behave! When we're at sea, dearest. *Then* we can have a little fun with her."

Sara released a sigh of relief. Had she detected a hint of jealousy in Alita's tone? Unlikely. She didn't like the sound of that "we can have fun with her" jibe.

Her empty stomach gyrated sickeningly. She had never been so helpless in her life. This was much worse than being held at gunpoint by Alita in Tenerife. Then she had been able to fight back.

Whatever relief she now experienced, it was crushingly temporary. She truly didn't want to contemplate the ordeal they had promised her.

Oh, Gene, this time I've made a complete mess of everything!

Rising from the bed, Belofsky wrapped an arm round Alita. "Let's leave her to think on what we have said."

Chapter 16

Jasmine Flower Revelations

Nanjing

Linghao drove Cat, Yubi and Rick in his minivan through the city and parked outside the *Mòlí Huà* bar. It was an unprepossessing place, a red neon sign above the door solely in Chinese, no windows and only one door, manned by a broad and sturdy bouncer. "This is where the two workers usually drink," Linghao said. "Its name is *Jasmine Flower*."

The bouncer nodded at Linghao, who spoke rapidly, doubtless vouching for them all, and the man then let them pass.

They entered a poorly lit dark passage; at the far end was a door. As they moved along, Cat detected a mixture of strong smells—tobacco, hashish, urine and cheap perfume, but no jasmine. As a chemist, she marveled that each odor was still distinguishable. Cat noticed Rick raise a hand to cover his mouth and nose. She sympathized; with his sensitive sense of smell, it must be demoralizing in here.

At the end of the passage, Linghao pushed open the door.

They entered the bar, a scruffy place, the floor littered with bits of paper litter and spittle.

She leaned close against Rick, whispered, "Even if the signs threaten fines, many people still tend to spit—maybe it's because of the serious air pollution affecting their throats. You'll get used to it."

"I doubt it," he replied.

"Whatever you do, don't go to the toilet," she warned.

"What if I need to?"

"Go if you must; only if you *really* have to. If you're lucky, it'll be a porcelain hole in the ground. You won't like it, I can assure you. Always go before leaving your hotel."

"Now she tells me. Sometimes, I wonder why I do this."

"Because you love me," she countered.

He gripped her hand, squeezed it. "That's the reason! I knew there was one."

Linghao led them past several groups of locals, all chatting loudly; a handful stared at the newcomers briefly, yet most didn't bother. He drew their attention to a stall occupied by three men. "That's Ying and the two men I told you about." He took a seat in the adjacent stall and they joined him. He leaned in to them, whispered, "Listen."

"Speak in English," someone said in the Ying booth, his voice grating. "In case anyone eavesdrops."

"That's Ying's voice; he's the factory chief," Linghao murmured. "You're in luck, I don't have to translate."

"What do you want?" Ying asked.

"We know about your smuggling project in Wuxi."

"I don't know what you're talking about." Ying sounded irate.

"Raw opium in those lucky cats."

Interesting! Guiltily, Cat clung tightly to her backpack.

Ying adopted a wheedling tone: "My business is here, in Nanjing."

"You've got a contact in Wuxi who happens to know my sister. They get to share notes. Pillow talk. You know how it is?"

"It is only talk, rumor. You have no proof."

"What about the murder of Heng?"

"Murder? Heng?"

Rick's hand clasped Cat's, tensed. He mouthed *murder* and muttered, "I think we should go, get out..."

Cat shook her head.

"Don't act so innocent," said the man. "The police have found his body. Song Chong is now involved."

"Song?" Ying queried. "Doesn't he work in Shanghai now?"

"We don't care where that man is or was, but we care about keeping you in circulation. Or we can always arrange for you to get an interview with the PSB..."

"You have no proof," Ying insisted. "I keep telling you!"

"We've been following you for a while, to be sure about you. Imagine our pleasant surprise when we saw you running away, still holding the gun."

"Smoking gun, eh?" said the other man.

"It is your word against mine," Ying insisted, though not convincingly.

There was the rustling of paper, which was flung down. "We photographed you with an iPhone—and it is definitely you, see, under the street light?"

Ying groaned. "What do you want?" Now his tone reflected defeat.

Cat stored that information. So Ying was probably arranging the smuggling without the knowledge of Dante. That made sense.

"Mr. Ying, we will keep quiet if you agree to help us."

"What kind of help?" Wary.

"Nothing too difficult: simply swap a shipment destined for Japan."

"What is the shipment?"

"Your factory's goji berry pills."

"But why swap them?"

"That's none of your business. Your secret is safe if you agree."

"If I agree, when do you want to make the swap?"

"Oh, you will agree. The exchange is to happen in the early hours of tomorrow morning. We know your latest output leaves the factory tonight. Arrange for your driver to go sick and use Li here... I will phone you with instructions about where we will leave your shipment, once we have made the exchange. You can always sell that shipment on, make a nice profit on the black market, no? We will then go to Shanghai with our replacement freight for delivery to the ship."

"How do I know you will keep your part of the bargain? After you've shipped the replacement pills, you could expose me."

"We could. Or we could use you again, perhaps?"

"I see... I have no option."

"That is right. You don't. Make sure that the paper-work is in order."

"Alright. The papers will be valid."

"Good."

The two men stood and all three now spoke in Mandarin. The two left the bar, and Ying followed a couple of minutes later. He was quite distinctive, wearing a red velveteen jacket with Mandarin collar and frog buttons; his white high collar shirt was worn outside the black trousers. Cat had glimpsed his thick dark eyebrows that slanted toward his nose, a high fore-head and a pencil-thin mustache.

"What are they planning?" Cat wondered aloud, standing.

Bing said, "It will remain a mystery—unless we identify the shipment they're talking about."

Cat made up her mind. "Yubi, go to the hotel with Rick. Bing, I need translators, will you and Linghao come with me?"

Rick gently gripped her arm. "Where are you going now?"

"We're going to follow them."

"You can't!"

"I must." She shrugged him off and made for the exit. Bing and Linghao reached her as she stepped outside.

She scanned the street. To her left, Ying lit a cigar and then began strolling along the path, shoulders hunched, talking into a cell-phone. To her right, she spotted the two men as they got into a black Qoros hatchback.

"We know where we can find Ying—at the factory," Cat said. "Let's trail your two fellow workers."

Linghao opened his minivan. "Get in, both of you!" Cat and Bing piled in and Linghao drew away from the curb in pursuit.

He drove through the city for about ten minutes, turned down a side street in time for them to observe the black hatchback pulling into a parking bay. A hotel's neon lights flickered, reflecting on the windshield.

Linghao parked next to the Qoros hatchback and they got out and followed the two men into the hotel, hovering in the foyer.

One of the men spoke to the receptionist; his voice echoed. The receptionist nodded, pointed to the elevator doors, and replied in Mandarin.

Cat squinted at Bing questioningly.

"She told them they're expected. Room 29," he translated.

The men crossed the foyer to the elevator; five floors were indicated. The men entered the elevator and it rose to the second floor.

Two more men entered the hotel and went straight to the elevator.

Linghao nudged Cat's arm, whispered, "I recognize those two. They don't work at the factory, but they were in the history group I attended."

"Perhaps they have extra-curricular history lessons?" Cat mused, watching the pair enter the open elevator cab.

"I think I could join them," Linghao suggested. "They'd know me from the group."

"Are you sure?" Concern in her voice. The elevator again stopped on the second floor.

"It is worth an attempt," Linghao said. "Here, keep my car keys in case you need to get away."

Before she could protest, another man entered the foyer and made for the elevator.

Linghao left her and Bing and hurried to join the newcomer.

After a tense delay of two minutes, the elevator arrived, the doors opened and Linghao and the man entered.

"What do we do?" Bing asked as the elevator doors closed.

"We use the minivan and return to the factory and wait for the truck to leave, and then follow it. We might see them switching the pills."

"Then what?"

"Follow if need be to the docks," Cat said.

"And what about Linghao? We can't leave him stranded here."

Chapter 17

The Long Fist

"Which floor?" the man asked in Mandarin, looking smart in his gray tunic suit with red piping.

"Second," Linghao replied, and felt sweat trickle down his neck, soak his collar. He anxiously wiped it with a hand.

"I don't know if you remember me, I'm Cheng," the man said as he pressed button 2. "I haven't seen you at our group's meetings for a while. Have you been ill?"

"No. Family matters—which kept me away, sadly. My name is Linghao." He could not risk using a false name, since those other two men knew him from work.

They both bowed briefly, formally.

"I hope we are not late," Linghao said, simply for something to say. He would have preferred to ask Cheng many questions but couldn't take that chance of exposing his ignorance. He must play along and hope to glean enough without being discovered as an agent provocateur.

Cheng looked at his watch. "No, we have a good five minutes. I got delayed in traffic."

"Traffic!" Linghao remonstrated. "It just gets worse!"

"It does—and the pollution. Ah, here we are."

The elevator stopped and the doors opened.

Boldly leading the way, Linghao made for room 29.

Once they arrived at the door Cheng reached past Linghao and pressed the doorbell.

The door opened. A lean bald man of about thirty stood in the doorway, barring their entry. "What did Wu Yuxiang say?" he asked of them both.

"The characteristic of the long fist is comparable to a long river," Cheng stated, and glanced sideways at Linghao, waiting.

Fortunately, Linghao knew the quotation and added, "Its waters run continuously and endlessly."

"Just so," the bald man said, nodding. "Revenge will be forever!"

Linghao and Cheng repeated in unison, "Revenge will be forever!"

"Welcome, late-comers!" announced a man in the middle of the lounge, clearly the center of attention. He wore a black tunic suit, the jacket opened to reveal a high-collared white shirt. He must be their leader, the way he held himself, shoulders back, chest puffed out, legs apart, a steady presence. He had a thin black mustache that curled to his chin; his black hair was swept behind his ears and tied in a short ponytail. The eyes were dark, glinting with a kind of inner-fire. Linghao didn't recognize him. Yet the man was obviously popular here. Standing next to him was a short studiously silent man in spectacles; he had a lean face and a pointed nose. He appeared to be in his sixties and wore a gray jacket and trousers.

As the leader's eyes scanned the assembled men— all men, not surprisingly—Linghao lowered his gaze. An instant later, he raised his head and the leader's focus was elsewhere. He released a breath and sensed his heartbeat slow down a little.

"As you know," the leader said, "some political groups and figures in Japan are still denying the barbarous crimes of Japanese aggression, and still paying homage to the souls of war criminals whose hands are stained with blood. But their time of true repentance is at hand!"

Cheng whispered, "He is formidable, Tang Kong, is he not?"

"Yes, mesmerizing," Linghao murmured.

"We are honored to follow him."

"We are indeed," Linghao affirmed.

"He will give us satisfaction at last," Cheng said, his concentration on Tang Kong.

Satisfaction regarding what? There were twelve present, besides him and Cheng. Some were probably staying in the hotel and had got here without venturing through the foyer. He'd been uncomfortable when his two fellow workers had attended the history group; now, he sensed a churning in his stomach that had nothing to do with hunger. It reminded him of times when he had inadvertently transgressed against official-dom. But this group was not official, had nothing to do with the government or any of its institutions. In fact it was subversive—and therefore dangerous. He wondered if the group had already been infiltrated by the PSB and they merely waited to pounce.

"Members of The Long Fist," Tang Kong exclaimed, "the day of *revenge* is close!"

Almost as one, those assembled raised an arm, fist in the air, and chanted, "The Long Fist!"

Linghao copied, only a few seconds behind them. Cheng, standing next to him, didn't seem to notice his hesitation or his unfamiliarity with their strange protocol.

At least he'd learned something: their group was called The Long Fist.

Tang Kong began reading from a booklet. It related the infamous attack and subjugation of Nanjing, the capital of China in 1937, by the invading Japanese. Their charismatic leader didn't spare them any of the gruesome details.

Linghao didn't need reminding; he knew all about it, as did almost every citizen. The first Nanjing Massacre Memorial Day was held quite recently on December 13, 2014; it had taken a long time to set aside such a day in the calendar, even though the actual memorial hall was built in 1985, near the site where thousands of bodies were buried in the "pit of ten thousand corpses". Both China and Japan officially acknowledged that wartime atrocities were committed, but there was still considerable divergence on the scale of this particular slaughter. And it still rankled that the Chinese had not received a suitable apology, only "deep repentance", which many believed was insincere and certainly inadequate.

No matter how much he knew, Linghao suffered a chill running through him as Tang Kong read out atrocity after atrocity.

It seemed that this recital was a ritual those assem-

bled underwent at each meeting. Repetition, reinforce-
ment: emphasizing the reason for their group's
existence. Justifying extreme hatred.

Several of those listening wailed at certain passages.

The massacre had gone on for days, not sparing
women, children or the men. Gang rape, beheadings
and bayoneting were the norm. Inhuman wasn't close
for the description of these events. Barbaric. He found
it inconceivable that so many could be murdered, their
bodies littering the streets. And yet he only had to look
at the history of the Soviet Union, the mass killings
ordered by Stalin. What he found difficult to comprehend was that it hadn't been medieval slaughter: this
had happened in the twentieth century. The torture
and the rape were as repugnant as anything the Nazis
had inflicted on their victims. And this was two years
before the Second World War. Of course the merciless
mistreatment of the Jews had been going on since the
early 1930s, long before war was declared. The inhu-
manity of both sides in the Spanish Civil War, which
was going on at the time, was merely a precursor for the
global carnage to come.

Linghao wondered if the land of the Middle Country, so soaked in blood, could ever again regain its
innocence.

"These horrendous acts will be *avenged*!" Tang
Kong declared. "We have worked tirelessly for many
years to prepare for this great *reckoning*! Now, Operation *Cataclysm* is at hand!"

While his insides roiled with anxiety, Linghao
followed the lead of Cheng next to him, wailing, and
cheering and laughing as appropriate. What did the
leader mean by "the day of revenge" and "this great

reckoning"? The name Operation Cataclysm didn't bode well...

"Our ancestors will be *avenged*," Tang Kong vowed. He continued to emphasize certain worrisome words. "Tonight, thousands of pills dispatched to Japan will be payment in full for the 300,000 of our men, women, and children massacred here in 1937!"

"At last!" wailed one man, tears glistening on his sunken cheeks.

"Revenge at last!" another cried.

Cheng shouted, "Revenge has been late in coming to fill our hearts and those of our loved ones!"

"Can you tell us how you have produced these pills?" asked another.

There were gasps of surprise and even concern. Who would dare question the leader?

Yet Tang Kong was unfazed. He gestured to the small bespectacled man standing next to him. "Dr. Fu Shen has worked on this program for three years. I will let him tell you."

Dr. Fu removed his glasses, wiped them with a white handkerchief. Squinting, he eyed those assembled and a thin smile spread across his face. His little dark eyes flashed. "Thanks to the donations from the many supporters of our cause, we constructed a smaller but similar factory. Over time we have obtained thousands of the genuine pills from the Ananke plant. The original coating has been replaced in our own manufacturing process. The printing of the packs has been done in the factory, also. Nobody could tell the difference in our product and that from the Ananke plant."

"What is special about the coating on the pills?" an elderly man asked, his tone more pragmatic.

Dr. Fu looked to the leader for guidance.

"It is a reasonable question," Tang Kong said. "Tell them, Doctor."

"Very well." Dr. Fu replaced his glasses. "The pill coating is a virulent carcinogen."

A few of the onlookers gulped audibly.

"Oh. Will it work?" the elderly questioner persisted.

Tang Kong glared. "Of course, yes."

"It will work, be assured," Dr. Fu confirmed.

Linghao was not too surprised about the existence of a shadow factory. Bing had told him of a number of cases involving foreign firms where the Chinese staff produced excess product and smuggled it out to sell on the black market at a reduced price; often, using blueprints, other factories were built but the finished product was inevitably inferior and eventually cost the original manufacturer in replacements. The fact that fraud was a capital crime didn't deter the culprits, either.

"But," interrupted another, "you will need more than 300,000 to infect that number. Stocks will stay on the shelves of pharmacies!"

"You are right!" Tang Kong said, grinning in approval. "We calculated on that and have prepared a million pills in the shipment. That should ensure our aim is achieved to infect *at least* 300,000."

Cheng interceded now. "But as soon as they know about the pills, they'll take them off the shelves— We—"

"Not so." Dr. Fu shook his head. "You forget, there will be no immediate effect, but within six to ten months, all those who ingest the pills will be riddled with terminal cancer."

"Ingenious," said the elderly questioner. "It is like a time-bomb, no?"

"That is indeed what we intend, yes," said Dr. Fu. "A slow fuse, if you will. Burning within."

Tang Kong smashed a fist into his palm "The havoc those pills will cause will be immense. And it will create untold grief. Grief we and our ancestors have had to shoulder for decades."

"The superior man takes three years to revenge an enemy; the common man has his revenge at once," intoned Cheng.

"It has taken us more than three years to exact our revenge, though!" snarled the elderly questioner, adding, "Yes, let them suffer the pain that our nation has endured for almost eighty years!"

Linghao's stomach felt rock hard, and there was shakiness in his limbs that he tried to control. He wanted to be sick.

The gleam in the eyes of all these men present seemed to reflect pure evil. He feared that he might stand out, not appearing fanatical enough. Yet they didn't seem to notice, they were too intent on their leader, Tang, too wrapped up in the deadly scheme.

"When will the consignment depart?" Cheng asked.

Tang squinted at his watch. "It left a few minutes ago and will soon rendezvous with the container it will replace. We are committed, members of The Long Fist! 'Operation Cataclysm' is under way as we speak!"

They all cheered and Linghao joined in while he sensed the sweat of fear running down his spine and soaking his shirt. He wanted to leave, get away, and warn the authorities, now that the dangerous pills were on their way.

He recalled that about ten years ago a fast food firm added dye to their food to make it look more appealing; they were unconcerned that the dye was carcinogenic. The adulteration of food was nothing new, he knew; it had been going on for centuries the world over—whether that was bread, sausages, butter, coffee or even milk. That and similar scandals forced the PRC government to create a new FDA authority that would monitor and enforce food safety. Whistle-blowers were now encouraged and rewarded by the Food and Drug Supervision Administration. But that was all about food and drugs, not healthcare products.

Besides, attempting to contact the authorities was not that simple. He didn't know the contact number to ring. Of course he could contact the Public Security Bureau direct. Yes, that was the best recourse. But he didn't have proof. By the time he convinced the PSB officers, it might be too late.

He consoled himself with the thought that there was no immediate threat to life. There was still time to put a halt to this lunacy.

LINGHAO EXITED the elevator and was met by Yubi, Rick and Bing. They explained that Cathy had taken his minivan and had gone on to the factory to track the consignment.

"But Bing, why are you here?" Linghao said. "Shouldn't you be with Cathy?"

"She sent me in a taxi to get Yubi and Rick and bring them here."

Linghao's brow furrowed. "Do we know where the consignment is likely to lead Cathy?

"To the docks, probably," Rick said, his tone morose.

"I don't believe this! She went alone!" Linghao said in alarm. "What was she thinking?"

"Tell me about it!" Rick snarled.

Linghao gripped Rick's arm. "I need to contact her, tell her what these people have planned. It is truly awful."

"If it's that bad," Yubi said, "shouldn't we tell the authorities now?"

Turning to her, Linghao exhaled in frustration. "If we had proof, yes, we should. But it is only hearsay."

"Tell us," Bing said.

"What have you heard?" Yubi demanded.

"I don't know if I want to hear this," Rick said.

Linghao told them.

Shanghai

Belofsky paced along the jetty while Alita stood at the foot of the gangway, vaping. This time she was smoking dragon banana berry, which he found sweet and cloying. Tersely, he exclaimed, "At last!" and thrust his arms in the air.

As before, the white unmarked van reversed toward the jetty and braked. The broad squat Chinese driver killed the engine and got out. He scratched his bald head. "Sorry I'm late. Traffic, you know how bad it gets."

Belofsky studied his watch. "Well, get on with it, man. We have an important event to attend tonight."

The driver bowed, opened the rear doors and let out his two relatives, each one carrying a polythene-covered bundle.

Turning to Alita, Belofsky said, irritably, "Show them where they are to put the merchandise."

She made a point of flinging the e-cigarette into the river, and then led the two men up the gangway.

When the driver had been paid and they had all left the jetty, Alita checked the blue face of her Marco Mavilla watch. "We have time, Anton. Shall we introduce Miss Whitney to her new friends?"

"Yes. But we mustn't linger, no matter how tempting. As you say, we can have our fun when at sea..."

SARA'S HANDCUFFS were unlocked and she awkwardly swung her legs round, and sat on the edge of the bed, rubbing her wrists and ankles. Fortunately, they released her whenever she needed to use the bathroom—or head, as he called it. And her hands were also freed to enable her to eat a cold pizza, but other than that she was shackled all the time, and the inflamed skin testified to that.

"Where are we going?" Sara asked, as Belofsky made her stand and clicked a separate pair of handcuffs on her.

"To see your new playmates," Alita answered.

Sara tried to push back, away from the door, but

Alita slapped her face hard, twice, to discourage her. "Don't make us angry, Miss Whitney. You won't like us when we get angry."

"I don't like you now, actually."

Belofsky arrested Alita's raised hand. "That's enough for now, dear."

"As you say," Alita snapped. "For now."

Sara exited the cabin. Alita went ahead. Belofsky was behind her, shoving her if she so much as faltered in her step.

They descended a stairway and walked along a passageway.

Her legs were a bit shaky after lying on the bed for what must have been hours—without her watch she had no idea how long, in fact.

Within a minute or so they came to a door on the left and another on the right.

Alita opened the left-hand door.

Belofsky shoved Sara inside and she came to a halt at the foot of a double bed. Lying on its covers were two attractive teenage girls, one black, the other Eurasian. They wore brightly colored dresses. Their eyes were shut, their chests gently swelling as they breathed in repose.

Sara's heart went out to them, for they were shackled in the same manner as she had been minutes earlier.

"What have you done to them?" Absently, she rubbed her wrists.

"Drugged," Alita said. "When they wake up, we can start to educate them."

"Educate?"

Belofsky looked with bemusement at Alita. "See, didn't I tell you? Delicious innocence!"

"You all need to learn how to provide pleasure for your clients," Alita explained.

Sara trembled and her stomach overturned.

"These girls are most fortunate," Belofsky said. "They're destined for a high-class brothel."

"You're despicable!" Sara snapped.

Alita playfully nudged him with her elbow. "I may thoroughly hate her, but I confess I do like her spirit!"

"And, my dear Miss Whitney," Belofsky added, "your fate will be somewhat different. You will go to comfort soldiers of the People's Republic of China..."

Chapter 18

Operation Cataclysm

Nanjing-Shanghai

Before leaving, Cat had slipped into the hotel bathroom to change into her black catsuit and trainers, tucking the cotton suit, blouse and Nike shoes in her backpack. Now, driving the minivan, she followed the truck from the factory, praying that it was the right one and that there were no other shipments dispatched tonight.

A short while later, she tailed the truck as it turned off at the G4011 cloverleaf and eventually pulled in at the well-lit Xianrenshan service area. Here, to one side of the restaurant building, the truck braked, parking next to an identical vehicle, even down to the markings on the container's side; only the license plates differed.

Cat parked the minivan in a nearby bay, from where she could observe the two vehicles without being noticed.

The driver of the truck she'd followed jumped to the ground and accosted the driver of the identical truck; they talked briefly and two envelopes changed hands. The new driver—presumably Ying's man named Li—got into his cab and started the engine. Having an identical commercial vehicle made the switch simple. Presumably, the new truck driver now had all the paperwork for the replacement container.

She pulled away and followed the replacement, which retraced the route back to the G42 expressway.

All the time, she drove warily, praying she was not stopped by traffic police for a slight misdemeanor. She was well aware that she couldn't master the language to fob them off and didn't have any documentation to prove she owned the van or was authorized to drive it. Maintaining a steady pace, she was determined to keep those tail lights in view; sometimes that meant swinging into another traffic lane to overtake, but at no time did she detect the presence of any police cars behind her. She felt sure that the truck driver wouldn't be able to identify any tail, either. All cats were the same color at night, she mused.

The road passed through tolls, wended past Chanzhou, then the outskirts of Wuxi, and Suzhou, all now familiar though previously seen from a different perspective and in daylight.

Most of the time she didn't concern herself with traffic direction signs, she simply followed the replacement container vehicle. She was lucky never to be caught by traffic lights.

Shanghai

Finally, the truck braked at the southern gate of Shanghai docks, joining a queue of two others.

Cat spotted a section of clear curb and turned the wheel and parked the minivan. Careful not to make any loud noise that would attract attention, she got out and quietly shut the door.

As she hurried toward the queue of vehicles, she spotted the driver of the first truck speaking to the man on gate duty. Paperwork was passed over, scrutinized and returned and the gate was rolled open.

The first truck drove through.

The sentry kept the gate open and beckoned to the driver of the next truck to move forward.

Cat peered over her shoulder. No other vehicles were approaching. Now she sprinted across the hardtop, heading for the rear of the replacement she'd been following, all the way wary not to appear in the rearview mirrors. Reaching the vehicle undetected, she slid smartly underneath its chassis. There was sufficient illumination from the floodlights that bordered the dockside fence for her to identify safe and firm hand- and foot-holds.

She swung herself up and held on tight, conscious of the dirt and grease that might swiftly jeopardize her grip. Free climbing mountains was a doddle compared to this.

An instant later, the truck moved forward and she was assailed by a strong smell of engine oil and warm exhaust. Quite familiar already. Then she almost lost her hold as the driver abruptly braked.

The man on the gate hadn't bothered examining the

undercarriage of the other trucks, so she gambled that he wouldn't do so with this one. She dropped her feet to the ground briefly to ease the tension and the weight on her arms.

She heard the sentry's footsteps approach the cab.

Rapid-fire Mandarin was shortly followed by the sound of the air-brakes being released.

Hastily, she resumed her position, finally jamming her left foot in.

The truck moved forward and she saw the passing shadows of the gate on the ground, and heard it trundle shut.

The truck wasn't moving fast—probably a low speed limit within the confines of the docks. Even so, the ground sped beneath her at a disquieting rate. And then she heard her cell-phone ringing in her backpack. She cursed—she should have switched it off or at least keyed it to silent mode. The truck cornered slowly and trundled over countersunk rail lines; laid for mobile cranes or gantries, she surmised.

In this fixed position, her shoulders and thighs were beginning to ache when the truck finally braked and juddered to a halt.

Quickly, she lowered herself to the road, scanned left and right, but spotted nobody's feet. She eased herself out from under the chassis, emerging on the driver's blind side. Getting to her knees, she raised herself to her feet and in a crouching lope hurried to a big patch of darkness a little way beyond the corner of the building the truck was parked alongside.

Catching her breath, she retrieved her cell-phone, checked its screen.

Missed call from Bing.

She rang him.

"Cathy, glad I caught you! Where are you?"

"Near the replacement container. At the docks right now. Why?"

"Linghao has discovered what is in the container, and it isn't good."

"Tell me."

He did, and on hearing his disclosure she slumped against the wall. "Oh, my God, Bing, that's terrible! It's mass murder."

"I know. They're calling it 'Operation Cataclysm'. Their reasons stem from almost eighty years ago. We should move on and not dwell on the atrocities of the past."

"I agree, Bing. But tell that to the Sunni and Shia, to the neo-Nazis, to the real IRA, to the extremists the world over... Hatred and anger is the breath of life to them."

"Such breath of life is warped, Cathy; it brings only misery and death."

"I know." She supposed that the Long Fist culprits would tell the world, eventually, to seek a kind of twisted vindication. "When the Japanese learn of the cause of those cancers, then the tension between China and Japan will increase. There'll be riots..."

"And perhaps much worse... What are you going to do?"

"I don't know, Bing. Obviously that shipment must be prevented from getting to Japan." She wondered if she'd known earlier, would she have contemplated ramming the truck? No, the minivan was no match; she'd have come off worse, for certain. It might have delayed the shipment long enough to organize the authorities, though. What might have been: that was wasted speculation.

The truck engine started and the brakes hissed.

"The container's on the move again. I'll call you when I can. Oh, and tell Rick not to worry!" She hung up, shoved the phone in her backpack and at a jog-trot followed the truck, sticking to the shadows.

The vehicle drove onto the dockside, dominated by a huge red crane resting in its countersunk rails. Security floodlights glared and played havoc with her night-vision.

To her left was a berthed container ship, its stern painted with QING JADE, SHANGHAI. Directly ahead, the brown-gray river reflected all the night lights from each side. Barges and tankers passed in both directions.

Now the driver of the truck climbed down, shouted to a longshoreman wearing a yellow hardhat. They'd be arranging for the container to get loaded, she supposed.

No matter. She now knew the name of the ship destined to carry the container. It was up to the authorities to stop it.

She removed her phone from the backpack and was about to contact Bing, when she stopped and stared. *Was this the luck of the waving cat?*

On the adjacent jetty to her right stood a pile of containers. A crane was already loading them onto another ship. The container that swung beneath the crane moved into the glare of floodlights and Cat recognized it immediately: it was the identification number C-WX-LC44 which she'd memorized from the Wuxi loading bay. It held those lucky cats and their illicit cargo of raw opium.

Must get the name of that ship too. Then the night's work would be done. Both shipments were from Ananke so Dante would yet again feel the ire of the law. But the name on the bow was partially obscured by a mixture of dirt and rust; all she could make out was ED TERN.

She shoved the phone into her backpack and walked briskly but not hurriedly, not wishing to draw attention to herself. Where possible, she clung to shadows. She began to walk the length of the ship.

"Ting zhu!" a man bellowed. *Oh, hell!* She recognized that cry as *Stop!*

She had no wish to answer questions now, even if the man spoke English. She spun on her heel and ran back along the jetty, again dodging in the shadows, until the silhouette of the man was no longer visible. Then, breathing easier, she moved forward, occasionally glancing over her shoulder, just in case.

Abruptly, she bumped into somebody who stood in the gloom. She stumbled back, bashing her shoulder against the ridged metal side-wall of a container. "Sorry!" she blurted, easing herself off and standing unsteadily.

"You are English?" the man, her obstruction, grated in English, discarding a cigar, its end glaring red ash.

"Yes... Sorry I bumped into you. I'm in a hurry..."

He took a pace into the light and she was unable to control the gasp of recognition she made. Ying stood before her, dressed as she'd last seen him, in a red velveteen jacket, complete with Mandarin collar and frog buttons, his white high collar shirt worn outside the trousers. His thick dark eyebrows slanted toward his nose, while his high forehead wrinkled.

"Do I know you?" he said.

"No." She glanced left and right, but whoever had shouted for her to stop must have given up. "I must be going."

He grabbed her upper arm, held her in a vice-like hold. "Wait, I think you are here for a reason."

"No, honestly, I'm trying to find a friend's yacht."

"Then you are going the wrong way." He thumbed over his shoulder, past the 'Ed Tern' ship. "The public berths are along there!"

"Thank you." She tried to prize his hand from her arm. "Will you let go of me, please?"

"I do not think so." With his free hand, he stroked his mustache in thought. "In fact, I do believe that you are spying on me!"

"That is preposterous! Let me go or I'll call the police!"

"Police?" He pulled out an automatic pistol from his jacket, pressed it against her side. "I do not think so."

"Please, Mr. Ying, why are you doing this?" Too late, she realized her mistake. She'd been too alarmed, had let his name slip out.

"So, you *do* know me, eh?" He pressed the gun even more firmly. Her mouth felt arid, her stomach gyrating. Cold and sick inside. This situation reminded her of the evil Zabala: he'd held a knife, and she'd disarmed him with taekwondo moves he hadn't expected. Now, Ying here had a gun on her and she stood no chance at all combating that weapon.

Fighting an unwelcome inability to speak, she decided she must distract him. "Yes," she croaked, "I know you." She cleared her throat. "We heard you talking to your friends. We know you killed Mr. Heng—probably with that very gun!"

Ying stepped back, pulling her with him, and snapped, "We? You said 'we'!" He looked behind him, left and right. "Who is with you?" he grated, his voice almost a scream.

"My friends..."

He let go of her, swung the pistol at her head.

She instinctively ducked so the full force of the blow missed her face and hit her shoulder. In the same instant, she side-kicked Ying's hip and then hit the ground and rolled away, skittering behind the container she'd bashed into.

Her breathing came fast and furious, while her hands felt damp and her knees and legs trembled. Taekwondo training combat was one thing; fighting for your life quite another. She didn't want to be shot. Well, she thought, who does, you stupid fool?

A quick appraisal told her she was in a kind of alley created by containers—and it was a dead-end.

Littering the ground was a pile of cigarette stubs, several coils of rope and an eight-inch long metal hook that protruded at a right angle from its wooden handle. Desperately, she grabbed the longshoreman's hook, held it so the hook stuck out between the fingers of her fist.

Not a moment too soon, for Ying's hand holding the gun appeared round the corner, then the arm. "That kick hurt!" he shouted. "You silly fool, you can't use martial arts against a gun!"

Taking a deep breath, she sliced out and down, impaling his gun arm with the hook.

Blood spurted, covered her hand, and Ying yelped.

The gun clattered to the ground.

Cat was shocked by the amount of the blood that flowed from the wound. Fearing he might pull her toward him, she let go of the hook's handle.

She was about to make a break from the "alley" when he moved forward, blocking her egress.

With his left hand holding his wounded arm, he harshly growled an expletive in Chinese, clearly something unpleasant. Unexpectedly, he kicked at her, a swift roundhouse. If it had connected, it would probably have crushed her skull. Instead, her reactions were quick and on overdrive. She darted to one side, away from him, and his foot slammed into the side wall of the container. She was sure it caused a dent; it probably didn't do his foot much good either.

He came at her in a rush now, limping a little, a front kick with his left foot, then his right, advancing at a dizzying rate. She backed away, sometimes protecting herself with a knife block, at others an x-block or an outer arm block.

In no time she was weary and sweaty, her arms bruised by the blocking moves she'd deployed.

His teeth clenched together, he grimaced. "You've got nowhere to run to!" he barked triumphantly.

She glanced over her shoulder. The locked doors of the container at the end of this alley were barely three feet away. It was darker here; dockside illumination didn't penetrate to any noticeable degree in this part of the "alley."

Ying limped forward and then stopped and stood still, breathing heavily, nursing his wounded arm, the handle of the hook protruding. Black dribbles fell to the ground; he was still bleeding. If he somehow extracted that hook and used it against her, she'd be finished.

He must have read her mind. "I'm going to skewer you with this!" he promised. Holding the hook imbedded in his arm, he moved toward her, his facial expression clearly betraying his intent to kill.

Cat backed off, half-turned and jumped up, and grabbed the door locking rail, an upright at the end of the box container that blocked off this "alley."

Ying's front kick missed, hitting air, while she used the rail for purchase and slammed both of her feet into his face. His eyes started, his mouth gaped open and he fell backward onto the ground.

She let go and landed on all fours; her forearms throbbed with the punishment they'd sustained.

Ying didn't move. Warily, she edged forward and knelt beside him. She fingered the pulse in his neck. Unconscious, not dead. Thank God for that, she thought, and then upbraided herself: the swine had intended killing her! Quickly now, she checked his wound; the bleeding was seepage, not spurting, so no punctured artery. She hadn't thought there was any chance of that, or he'd probably have been dead by now.

Casting about, she spotted his fallen gun. She recalled Chuck's constant mantra, "Fingerprints, always think fingerprints!" So she delved in her back-pack and used a pair of her knickers to retrieve the weapon. Carefully, she shoved the automatic in his pocket and replaced her briefs Then she selected several pieces of rope from the ground and tied his hands together, attaching them to the locking rail. Finally, she lashed his ankles together, and then tested the tautness of the bonds and the strength of her knots, though it pained her wrists to do so. When he regained consciousness, he wouldn't be able to get free. Trussed up for the police, in due course.

"Mr. Song, you asked me to get in touch if the Ananke security cameras detected anything." He recognized the caller-ID. It was Ruan Peng, the master of the *Qing Jade*.

Song sat up, immediately alert. "Yes, what have you found?"

"Facial recognition has identified the woman you recently input into the system. She walked past my ship about ten minutes ago."

Ten minutes! She was within his grasp, he felt sure now. "Have you sent anybody to locate her yet?"

"No, sir. I decided to wait for your instructions."

"Very good." The fact that she was on the dockside boded ill, Song thought. She must be attempting to sabotage the shipment of Wuxi goji pills. "I will come to the docks. What time do you sail?"

"In two hours' time, sir."

"When I get there, show me the security camera video."

"Yes, sir, I will prepare it in readiness."

After a minute, Cat's breathing was under control. She could leave—no, she couldn't; not easily, anyway. She'd hitched a ride in here. She couldn't account for her presence. The sentry would have to get in touch with his superiors, and probably involve the police, and combine those delays with the very real problem of the language, and she might not be able to alert anyone in authority about the two consignments before the ships sailed. Even if they believed her. Well, she still had the package of raw opium in her backpack. Ying lying here was good evidence, too; he was the perpetrator, the brains behind the opium smuggling. And perhaps the gun was the same weapon that killed Heng. But all that would take time. She had no evidence regarding the adulterated goji berry pills. At the very least, she needed the name of the ship; it certainly wasn't *Ed Tern*.

Reluctantly, she retraced her steps back toward the ship, hoping that the man who had shouted *stop* to her had gone.

She was not stopped and finally reached the jetty at the stern of the ship. This was the last commercial vessel berthed on the dockside. Further along was a fence with a locked gate, a notice reading, in Chinese characters and also in English, PRIVATE BERTHING ONLY. Beyond, past the fence five luxury cruisers were moored. On that side of the fence was a two-story building with external stairs; its wide glass windows were black. Probably the harbor master's office.

On the stern of the ship she read: RED LANTERN, SHANGHAI.

That was enough. Now she could phone Bing, start the wheels turning. Relief flowed through her. It was finished. She'd done enough. Now, get out of the docks. Maybe the best way was to clamber over the fence; the public section of the jetty might not be so strictly guarded or monitored.

She strode to the wire mesh fence, which was about

eight feet high. The top of it was strung with razor wire. It would slice through any clothing she used to protect her hands and body. The fence ran to the edge of the jetty, where it was constructed with long vicious-looking metal spikes placed specially to thwart any trespasser who considered clambering round from one side to the other. The alternative was to get wet, and judging by the mess of plastic and vegetable flotsam clinging to the pilings, she didn't fancy immersing herself in that glop. There was a locked gate halfway along the fence.

She froze, drawn by voices that came from the luxury cruiser in the middle of those five.

A man and a woman descended that boat's gangway, heading toward a waiting black limousine. Briefly, they strolled into the down-glare of a floodlight and she had no difficulty identifying them both. *My God!*

She recalled the photos Lieutenant Vargas had shown her in Tenerife.

Like a caged beast she cat-footed along the fence, focusing on them to make sure.

As she got closer, there was no doubt in her mind: Anton Belofsky and the escaped murderess, Alita Lopez!

Chapter 19

Curious Cat

S ong showed his pass at the commercial gate and was waved through. He drove straight to the dockside and braked beside a pile of containers, not many yards away from the foot of the gangway to the *Qing Jade,* where Captain Ruan Peng stood smoking a cigarette.

He switched off the engine, climbed out and walked over. They bowed respectfully to each other. "I got here as fast as I could," Song said. "Thanks for being so alert."

Ruan was stocky, with a mustache, a peaked cap at a jaunty angle, and a tobacco-stained smile. He dropped the cigarette to the ground and stood on it firmly. "Don't praise me. Save it for my communications officer. He is most thorough."

"Good man. Did you post a sentry at the top of the gangway?"

"As you suggested. No unknown person—man or woman—boarded the *Jade* by the gangway," Ruan said emphatically.

Song looked at the hawsers that tied the ship to the jetty's bollards. "I see you have put out the rat-guards, so she couldn't have climbed up those and negotiated round them, either."

Ruan stroked his mustache. "She's capable of doing that, is she?"

"Oh, yes. An accomplished free climber, among other things, I believe." He clapped Ruan on the shoulder. "You'd better show me the video."

"It is ready for you, Mr. Song. Follow me." Ruan swung round and ascended the gangway, Song a pace behind him.

WHEN THE LIMOUSINE had driven away, Cat unslung her backpack and then slowly climbed the mesh fence with ease. She'd examined the gate's lock and it was modern; it would take her longer to pick it than it would to scale the fence.

When she was eye-level with the top, she carefully placed the backpack on the razor wire and tentatively pressed on it with one hand. The tough material withstood the pressure and the razor wire didn't appear to cut into it. That may be a false sense of security, though, since it was only the weight of her hand pushing down. She'd have to be slick about this. If she slipped, she could lose a limb or sever an artery.

In truth she felt "pumped", a burning sensation in her forearms, a feeling familiar to her during climbing. But the burning was due to the serious blows Ying had delivered, not her straining on any rock face.

Was this a risk too far? She could go back, attempt to get through the commercial entrance.

Seeing Belofsky and Lopez in the flesh brought it to vivid recall. She remembered Howard on his death-bed, and steeled herself. She must try, for Howard's sake.

The crux of this particular climb was balance and coordination.

Shakily standing with her feet inserted in the mesh, she leaned forward, half-turned and put both her hands on the backpack. Balancing, steadying herself, she edged her feet out of the mesh, on tiptoes, and was pleased to note there was no wobble yet; the gate was more solid than a fence.

Now for it! Exerting her weight on her hands and shoulders, she thrust her hip over, legs following. She immediately let go of the backpack as she sailed above the top of the fence.

Once clear, she twisted round in mid-air.

Catlike, she landed on all fours, and hardly made a sound.

Quickly, she scaled this side of the fence and retrieved the backpack. The razor wire had cut into it and ruined her change of clothing and one of her latex gloves; fortunately, it hadn't completely cut through to the other side, or she'd have been sliced and diced by now.

The side-pockets of the backpack were intact and still held her tools and the package of opium was undamaged. If she could hide the drug on Belofsky's boat and then arrange an anonymous tip-off, he'd definitely get arrested for drug-running.

She hurried up the gangway and trod silently onto

the main deck. Standing stock still, she removed the intact latex glove and put it on her right hand.

The glass doors were locked but the lock-pick soon got her inside.

Dockside lights penetrated, provided adequate illumination.

Passing the bar on her left, she moved quietly into the dining area, listening attentively all the while. A bedroom seemed a good place to hide the opium.

She hoped the door ahead led into the master bedroom cabin. She opened the door and switched on the light. It was luxurious, complete with a TV set at the foot of the bed.

Where best to hide the opium? Not too obvious, it mustn't look like it was planted—but it must be found in a search.

Tentatively, she opened the door opposite, which led her into a compact office area, with a table, two chairs, a computer, a printer and a bureau.

Opening the bureau, she found letters, bills, receipts, blank writing paper, a letter opener, scissors, adhesive tape, pens and a Samsung tablet.

She slid the package from her backpack. Hurrying to the bathroom, she used a towel to wipe the package to remove her fingerprints.

She surveyed the bedroom and spotted a glass tumbler on each side of the bedhead. Returning to the office area, she crossed to the bureau and took the adhesive tape and carefully used it to peel off a couple of fingerprints from each tumbler and transfer them to the opium package. She scrunched the sticky tapes and pocketed them.

A small drawer in the center of the bureau

contained about twenty color photographs of young women in various stages of undress; all of them were shackled to beds and their faces reflected fear and, in some instances, disgust.

Cat put the package in this drawer and covered it with the photographs.

As she shut the drawer and then the bureau, she was about to turn and hurry out, her task complete, when a phone trilled, the sound coming from behind the next door.

Her heart began to pound.

Somebody in there!

She must get out, and quick.

"*Oh, Gene!*" a woman exclaimed.

Speaking English? Gene? Gene Brin? Was he here?

She knew that Chuck would advocate she left fast, but an insistent sixth sense impelled her to learn as much as she could. It was irresistible. Curious cat.

Hoping it wouldn't be the death of her, she opened the door and stared.

Sara was handcuffed to a bed. Nobody else was in the cabin.

Sara's eyes started as she recognized her. "Cathy! How...?"

"Later, Sara." Cat hurried to the bedside. "Let's get you out of here!"

"Belofsky and Lopez have gone for the evening—to the oil symposium. We should have more than enough time, don't worry." Sara rattled her handcuffs. "But they probably took the keys with them."

"No problem." Cat took her lock-pick and used it on the right-hand cuff. It clicked and she opened it, freed Sara's wrist.

"You must teach me how to do that!"

"A better approach might be trying not to get hand-cuffed again," Cat said, releasing Sara's left wrist. "Did they harm you?"

Sara sat up, touched the bruise on her forehead. "No, they were saving me for their 'fun' at sea..."

"That Lopez woman's really twisted."

Shortly, Cat had freed the cuffs on Sara's ankles.

She put the lock-pick away while Sara slipped on her shoes and attempted to stand. After a moment or two of trial and error, she managed it, supporting herself with one hand on the wall. A little shakily, she tottered to the dressing table, retrieved her cell-phone. "Three missed calls—all from Gene!"

"Ring him back and tell him to come for you at the public berth entrance gate. He should try to get in touch with the port authority so you can be let out."

"What about you?"

"That's a bit awkward. Officially, I'm not here."

"Couldn't Gene vouch for you?"

"That's a possibility. Right now, though, I need to phone my people too." Rick would be really anxious by now.

Sara got through to Gene at once and Cat could hear his exclamation of anger mixed with joy. When she mentioned Cat, the other end of the line quietened.

Sara looked at Cat, shrugged, and smiled. "How soon can you get to the public gate with someone who speaks the language?" Sara asked. She listened then said, "Okay. See you in twenty minutes. Love you." She switched off.

Cat used her phone and contacted Rick and braced herself for recriminations.

"Cathy, where the hell are you? You were supposed to be following—"

"I did—and I've got all the information we need. I'm at the dockside on Belofsky's boat right now."

"What!"

"It's alright, neither he nor Lopez are here."

"What the hell are you doing, Cathy?"

"Can you put Bing on, please? I need to explain to him."

Annoyed silence and then Bing's voice: "Hi, Cathy. Rick's really pissed off, you know. We're all worried about you."

"I think you'll agree it has been worth the worry, Bing. Listen."

Succinctly, she told him about the opium planted on the boat, and Ying tethered amidst the containers. "Ying definitely killed Heng, the security officer of Nanjing. His gun is in his pocket."

"Oh, my God," whispered Sara.

"And," Cat went on, ignoring the anxious look on Sara's face, "the container with the opium is on the ship *Red Lantern*, bound for Tenerife. The adulterated pills are on the *Qing Jade*, destined for Tokyo. Got that?"

"*Red Lantern*—opium. *Qing Jade*—pills. Yes. What—?"

"Wearing your journalist's hat, can you start the wheels turning to prevent them sailing?"

"You're asking a lot, Cathy. I have little to no clout, but I'll try. Oh, here's Rick again."

"What are you going to do now?" Rick demanded.

"I'll be at the public entrance gate, not the commercial one, waiting with Sara Whitney. We're expecting Gene to be there in about fifteen minutes."

"Sara? Gene? They're here?" His tone lightened and she could imagine him smiling now. "Well, that's great, love. I'll be there soon, too. Sorry I shouted."

"I'll think of something to make it up to you, promise." She switched off.

Sara's face brightened in amusement.

"Well, Sara, let's go and meet Gene."

Slipping her phone in her handbag, Sara paused, and then exclaimed, "Oh, God, I forgot—those poor girls!"

"Girls, what girls?"

"Belofsky's got a couple chained to the bed like me on the next deck down—they're drugged." She made for the door, paused. "We've got to help them!"

"Show me."

Leading the way, they descended to the cabin deck and Sara unerringly found the door, opened it.

Cat pushed past her and knelt on the bed and checked the two teenagers. Both were still drugged, but there was nothing wrong with their breathing.

She got off the bed, slid past Sara and crossed the passage and opened the door opposite. Inside this cabin were two more girls, also shackled and drugged. She turned to Sara. "We can't take them with us now. But once the authorities are informed, they'll be released."

Sara had paled at sight of these other two. "I was going to be one of them, you know. Alita Lopez said so."

"Not anymore," Cat said. "Gene will soon be waiting. We need to move."

"Yes, of course." Casting a glance at the supine girls, Sara then headed along the passage and up the stairs. "Follow me, Cathy. I know the way well; it's all I had to visualize while lying in that damned cabin."

Minutes later, they emerged on the main deck and crossed the gangway onto the jetty.

Sara breathed a sigh of relief. "I'm glad that ordeal's over!"

"What ordeal would that be, Madam?" a man said, his body silhouetted by a light at his back. He had a bullet-head, unusually long arms, big hands and broad shoulders.

He was alone, Cat noted.

Sara stared, surprised. "Who...?"

"It's Mr. Song," Cat said, recognizing him from the time he stood shaking his fist outside Yubi's house. "How did you find me?" she asked him.

"Cameras detected you—showed you passing the *Red Lantern*, coming here. You seem to have been busy. I presume this isn't your luxury cruiser?"

"No, it belongs to a Russian oligarch."

"Really? And who is this with you? The cameras never showed her."

"This is a friend I was helping ashore. She has nothing to do with Ananke or Dante. Her partner's waiting for her at the gate, in fact."

"Then don't let me delay her," Song said.

"Sara, go to the entry gate. Rick is coming with my friend Bing and they will make sure the girls below get help."

"Aren't you coming with me?"

"No. I've got to speak to Mr. Song here."

"Will you be alright? If he were to harm you..."

"She will be alright," Song said. "I have no wish to do Catherine harm. And I have no quarrel with you."

Sara hesitated. "Quarrel? If you have any kind of quarrel with Cathy, then I'm staying with her."

"Sara, please go!" Cat urged, shoving her gently.

Anxiety on her face, Sara gave a darting look at Song, turned and ran in the direction of the entrance, her shoes loud on the hard concrete.

Song took a step closer, unthreatening. Light now revealed his features. Cat found it difficult to guess the age of Chinese and Japanese; perhaps he was in his thirties. He was imposing, six feet four, she reckoned, muscular and barrel-chested, with a golden complexion and an inscrutable gaze from almond eyes. His nose was pug, with high-cut nostrils.

Cat faced him. "Did you mean that, about no harm?"

"That applied to your lady friend only. Mr. Dante wants your blood—well, a sample of it. Let me take that and then please agree to remain with me while we get the results, and I assure you that you will not come to any harm."

"I can't do that," she said.

"Then, I fear that you might come to some harm, after all. Only a little."

Chapter 20

"*Dante has won!*"

S ong maintained a relaxed stance, but she wasn't deceived. His feet were spread apart, taking his weight, as if about to begin a karate kata or taekwondo form. "You realize that I cannot let you go." It was a statement, not a question.

Cat looked behind her. Sara was out of sight. It was possible that she could return any minute with help, perhaps accompanied by the gate sentry or even police. If she could delay Song long enough, it was a slim hope to cling onto. Behind him was the fence, the gate now open, and a little way further along, his car. The loading continued for both container ships, the longshoremen unaware or unconcerned about her predicament.

Or I can run, she thought. Her instructor Mark was clear on that point. Run if you can, rather than fight. Fighting was always a last resort.

"Don't think about running after your friend." He must be a mind-reader. "I assure you, I am fleet of foot."

She believed him. His thigh muscles bulged against

the fabric of his trousers. Those long arms and big hands gave him an advantage, too.

Treat this as an exercise, she told herself. She was emboldened by the fact that he wanted her alive and preferably in one piece, so any blows he might administer would be the equivalent of sparring.

Slowly, she bowed to him, maintaining eye contact.

Song returned the gesture, a slight curve of his lips suggesting amusement.

He moved forward, huge fists raised to chest height, his body sideways on to her. "I will make it quick," he promised.

Over-confident? Or just very good?

He would use his superior reach, attempt to punch her.

She closed the distance, taking a step forward on her left foot and immediately attacked with a roundhouse kick to his torso. Her move usually startled the opponent into immobility so she could attack again.

But Song was fast, leaning away as she threw the kick. So she followed up with an unexpected reverse punch aimed at his chin.

If it had connected, it might have dazed him. His forearm block was firm and efficient.

She backed off, not wanting to get within the grasp of his long arms.

All of her forearm tingled with the force of his defensive block.

Unlike Ying, Song wasn't using any kicking techniques. She suspected that was because he could do a lot of damage with those muscular thighs and leather shoes, and refrained on purpose. Her trainers would not hurt as much on contact. He wanted her intact, which was no consolation.

He advanced on her, thrusting his long arms in one forward punch after another, and she darted out of the way for some thrusts and for others had no choice but to block repeatedly with her forearms.

In a short while her already badly bruised arms felt numb.

He was wearing her down, she knew. And his punches were getting closer. His onslaught was persistent, consistent, and brutal.

She must kick, use the kicking attacks, to avoid those arms.

Time lost meaning as she circled him.

Watching her, slowly moving to keep eye contact, he gave a wide grin, and for the first time she noticed his sharp teeth. Did he file them? She shuddered.

"If you think you're killing time while help comes, then you will have to try harder. So far, you have only taken four minutes to achieve very little."

Four minutes!

Was he goading her? Well, she wasn't going to consult her wristwatch.

She moved into the attack again, driving Song back with a rear-leg fake kick. As he took a short step backward, Cat prepared to launch a rear-leg front kick. But Song detected her intention and moved to the rear and changed posture, blocking the kick with a forearm that hurt her shin. She was thrown by his quick response and checked her kick. Her moment of indecision was all he needed and he counter-attacked with a rear-leg roundhouse kick to her temple.

She felt and heard the blow and her vision was

instantly blurred. Her head ached. But she backed away, wiping her knuckles against her forehead; they were smeared with her blood. *Bastard!*

She blinked away the tears and the pain. Perceived him standing, waiting.

Movement behind him distracted her fleetingly and her heart sank as she perceived that both ships were casting off their hawsers, leaving their berths, slowly moving out into the river. She groaned.

"Had enough? Will you come quietly?"

"No!" She attacked, attempting a rear-leg round-house kick.

Song blocked efficiently as he took a step to the rear.

Cat then attempted another rear-leg roundhouse to take advantage of Song's changed defensive posture.

Gallingly, he side-stepped and blocked her attack with one arm and followed through with the other, landing a punch to her solar plexus.

Bending in pain, heaving in air, she sank to her knees and vaguely she sensed one of his big hands grasp her neck. There was nothing she could do to stop him throttling her, she knew. Pain swamped her; it was so severe it paralyzed her.

He applied pressure and her view of the world diminished into a black spot and then nothing.

Rome

Sitting on the outside veranda of Caffè Oppio, Gilda Turati studied the Colosseum floodlit in all its ancient glory. Below in the street motor scooters buzzed and people shouted and chatted. Here, the hubbub was light, friendly, the waiters and waitresses dressed in black being efficient and friendly. The dessert dishes had been cleared and she and Luigi fondled their wine glasses. "Fondled", hmm? She knew Luigi desired to fondle her; her attraction was emphasized by her vibrant sapphire jersey dress, its neckline of matt sequins drawing attention to her cleavage. Most of the evening he'd had difficulty raising his gray eyes from her chest.

"The wedding is planned for next month," she said. Luigi was handsome and he knew it. But he had brains, too. In fact, she reckoned he had everything. And soon he would have her. Though on her own terms. "So, Luigi, once I've enjoyed the raptures of my honeymoon, how soon can you get rid of Dante for me?"

He trailed a hand over his chin, the designer stubble bristling. "I was under the impression that you loved him?"

"I do—after a fashion."

"Oh..."

"Fashions change. I love you, really."

"I know. I was only teasing."

"Don't tease—this is serious business."

"Is he going to agree to write a new Will?"

She rested her be-ringed hand on his. "We have discussed it. I will sign mine, he will sign his. There won't be any pre-nuptial agreements. Whoever survives the marriage gets *everything*!"

He raised her hand to his lips, kissed her knuckles, an action that sent a frisson of pleasure through her, tensing her stomach and groin.

"You're so enticing, Gilda. I can understand how he would do anything for you."

He leaned across and kissed her neck. A brief gesture, but the touch of his lips on the skin above her carotid artery sent a tingle into her brain.

With an effort, she sat back and controlled her breathing. "Our time will come, Luigi."

"You realize that when you have his business, the Turattis will be bigger than all the families in Rome?"

"Not only bigger, my love, but stronger."

Luigi Goretti winked at her. "That as well."

Shanghai

Cat regained consciousness and gasped as the pain hit her anew. It wasn't helped by Song carrying her over his broad shoulder. Each step he took was agony, jarring her whole body. She was lathered in sweat and her limbs felt terribly weak. Tears induced by the pain streamed down her cheeks. The overwhelming throbbing ache meant she could hardly think straight.

They passed through the gate in the fence that she'd climbed a short while earlier. Now, she doubted she'd be able to stand, let alone climb. She craned her neck awkwardly and saw his car parked a short way beyond, close to the containers where she'd fought Ying.

Song walked past the trussed figure of Ying, who was still unconscious. "I noticed him when I came this way. Did you do that?"

"Yes," she croaked. "He admitted to killing the Nanjing security officer, Heng."

"He did, did he? Nice work, Catherine," he said, a note of admiration in his voice, which surprised her. "Police Inspector Hou and his sergeant Yu will be very pleased to apprehend Mr. Ying." He chuckled. "It will get them off my back, too!" With his free hand, he pulled out his phone.

There was a garbled response on his phone and then he spoke briefly in Mandarin.

She hadn't a clue what he said but assumed it boded ill for Ying, which was no bad thing.

He ended the conversation, pocketed the phone and a short while later he reached his car and she realized that he was alone, without the two henchmen who had accompanied him at Yubi's. Maybe that was for the best; she guessed that one of them at least might not look too kindly upon her, after she had given him such a sore head.

He used the remote to unlock the car and then opened the door, lowered her onto the rear seat. "If I asked you to stay and promise not to attempt to escape, would you do that?"

"No," she replied, though speaking pained her. "Sorry."

He shrugged those big shoulders. "I thought not." His hand swiftly darted toward her head, struck her temple and everything went black for a second time.

GENE EMBRACED SARA, overjoyed to find her unharmed. Beside him was Daphne, who had talked the gate sentry into opening up. The sentry smiled at Daphne, as if smitten.

Shortly, Rick arrived with Yubi, Bing and Linghao. Bing explained that he'd hired a car and they'd found Linghao's minivan near the commercial gate.

Rick waved at them in greeting, his eyes darting. "Where's Cathy?"

Sara thumbed anxiously behind. "She—she stayed behind to talk to a Mr. Song. She said it was alright."

"Song?" The color drained from Rick's face.

"Is he the man you told me about?" Bing asked Yubi.

Tight-lipped, she nodded, moisture now brimming her eyes.

Rick swore under his breath. "What do we do now?" he moaned.

Bing stepped forward, gripped Rick's shoulders. "We must get in touch with the authorities and tell them about the shipments."

"But we have no proof!" Rick gritted his teeth.

"There's the man Ying that Cathy mentioned," Bing said. "He is linked to the opium." He turned to the gate sentry and chatted for a full minute. Reluctantly the man agreed that Bing could use the office telephone.

"I hope I can find someone to believe me!" Bing said and followed the sentry inside.

Gene followed and said, "Let's try Mr. Kuang."

Rome

Gilda caught the flight to Shanghai. She wasn't looking forward to the twelve-hour journey and had dressed for comfort in a white silk blouse, a Pierotucci white nappa lambskin jacket and black silk trousers.

It would be good to see Loup again, and he would be surprised to see her. She had already arranged with his secretary to delay his flight to Rome by a day, so they could have time together in his hotel.

She licked her lips in anticipation. He was most attentive to her needs. She'd miss that, she supposed, when the time came. Luigi was younger, more virile, but sometimes he neglected to show her how much he loved her. It did cross her mind that perhaps Luigi was playing her game, and intended devouring the Turati business empire. He'd have a problem there, though. She would be his woman, but she would not marry him.

Shanghai

Gene had memorized the number on the business card and got in touch with Mr. Kuang. The port official was shocked to hear what Gene had to say and he arrived twenty minutes later.

Introductions were made and once Sara had explained the situation, Mr. Kuang authorized their entry under his supervision. The sentry was happy to oblige.

By the time they reached the place where Sara had left Cathy, Cathy was no longer there.

Rick stood with drooped shoulders and his face appeared forlorn. "Song's taken her!" he grated.

"That is a serious accusation, Mr. Barnes," Mr. Kuang said. "Kidnapping is a capital offence."

Rick looked away in despair. "Dante has won!"

Awkward silence followed his outburst and then Mr. Kuang said, "I suggest you all return to the hotel. I will look into the information you have given me and get in touch when I learn something."

"When or if?" Rick snarled.

"Come on, there's nothing we can do here," Bing said, forcefully taking Rick's arm.

INSPECTOR HOU LIAISED with Shanghai's Inspector Bai and both arrived at the gate to the commercial docks.

Their vehicles were passed through and pulled in alongside a pile of containers.

Their sergeants scoured the area and Yu dashed back, shouting, "We've found Ying, sir. He's coming round now."

All four men strode past several containers and turned into the "alley."

At the far end was Ying, tied to the container doors, shaking his head, clearly looking befuddled.

Sergeant Yu put on latex gloves and searched Ying. Gingerly, he lifted from a pocket an automatic pistol. "Exhibit A, sir."

"Eh?" Ying said as he fully regained consciousness. "Police... What are you doing here?"

CAT REGAINED CONSCIOUSNESS IN A BASEMENT, her hands tied behind her back and secured to a metal chair. Reminiscent of Yubi's predicament, she thought. She was surprised that she felt no pain; yes, she ached, but that terrible ache in her solar plexus area had gone entirely. She was still fully clothed, she noted. Even so, she was uneasy about having been at Song's mercy while unconscious. The only time she'd been unconscious was with alcohol, when she was in Uni at Newcastle, having drunk too many gins and blacked out. Yubi had been there with her, fortunately, but that ghastly experience convinced her that allowing herself to get into a situation where her body was no longer under her control was not only foolish, but dangerous. She hadn't touched gin for years afterwards, the smell alone enough to repel her. Her taste for other drinks was not affected, however.

Song was on the telephone, speaking in English. "I will do that now, Mr. Dante. Have them send the courier round in ten minutes." He sat on an upright chair beside a long table pushed against a wall; and on it she saw a computer tower and screen, a microwave, a small fridge, a compact freezer and a kettle, mugs, plates and plastic cutlery, as well as the landline telephone with its speaker box.

The basement was spacious, with no windows. There were two bunk beds, each against a different wall. Her backpack lay on a sofa. A small television on a stand showed a colorful Beijing opera with the sound muted. Over her shoulder she glimpsed a workbench cluttered with medical packs of various shapes and sizes. On the floor by the table was a black plastic bag, half-full with empty microwave meal boxes. Her stomach rumbled.

Opposite the access door was another door, which

was partly open, allowing her to glimpse the bathroom. She wondered what the basement was used for and then decided not to dwell on that.

Song lowered the phone onto its cradle, rose and walked up to her. "This is not personal, Catherine. It shouldn't hurt." He reached behind her and produced a hypodermic syringe in a sealed packet. He tore open the packet and with his free hand gripped the shoulder seam of her cat-suit and tugged severely, ripping the sleeve so that it bunched at her elbow. He held a cotton swab, dabbed her arm, and she experienced a slight coolness, and then he expertly inserted the needle.

The pin-prick was slight, but it was without her consent: a gross invasion of her personal space, her body.

"See, hardly hurts at all." He gave her a smile, his teeth sharp and threatening.

"The pain I experienced, it has gone," she said. "Did you drug me?"

"No. I applied my fingers to a couple of your pressure points. I'm pleased the technique worked to relieve you of the pain."

"Thank you." She watched her blood fill the glass barrel of the syringe.

When the barrel was full, he eased the needle out, swabbed the area again. "There, all done."

He strode to the workbench, opened a small plastic box, placed the syringe inside amidst cotton wool, then closed the lid, clicked it shut. There was a label on the box but at this distance she couldn't read it.

A door-bell rang upstairs. "That will be the courier," he said. "I won't be long—amuse yourself while I'm gone."

Chapter 21

Beretta and Flowers

A police people-carrier parked next to Inspector Bai's vehicle at the docks and Ying, now handcuffed, was put inside. Inspector Bai's cell-phone rang and he swung round, away from Inspector Hou, and said, "Excuse me." He listened and then closed the call, and shook his head.

"Is there a problem?" Hou asked.

"Possibly. It seems it is all happening here on the docks tonight. We've had a tip-off that there's an opium smuggler on one of those luxury boats there." He gestured beyond the fence at the public berths. "I'm awaiting more details. In the meantime, I suggest you accompany your prisoner to the station, while I continue this new investigation?"

"That will suit me, Inspector Bai." Hou bowed slightly and bawled for his sergeant. They got in the front of the police van and then it drove away.

Inspector Bai told his sergeant, "I fear that it is going to be a long night."

AFTER THE OIL SYMPOSIUM CONCLUDED, the audience left the hotel conference room and entered the entertainment lounge, spreading among the tables covered with white cloths. Bottles of wine, chillers and glasses with plates of hors d'oeuvres were placed at each table.

Belofsky and Alita Lopez weaved through the throng. A frisson of pleasure scurried through her as she sensed several men's eyes on her. The symposium had been boring, but the night was young yet; it was bound to liven up. Her Ralph Lauren gown had a ruched body that draped over her right shoulder, accented by a jewel-encrusted brooch. The spandex material and the slit to thigh enhanced her figure, while the blush color complemented her complexion. In contrast, she carried a red calfskin Hermès clutch bag.

Anton selected a table at the front, a couple of paces from the stage.

The stage was quite low, maybe a foot high. A Chinese cabaret singer gave a rendition of "Memory" from the show *Cats*; Alita reckoned that she remembered a fair portion of the lyrics, anyway. Most of the watching men were not interested in the words, she reckoned.

Settling into her seat, Alita looked at Anton. His face was flushed. He appeared to have eyes only for the singer whose tight-fitting cheongsam blatantly emphasized her voluptuous figure. But she knew that his smile was not reserved for the chanteuse; he was pleased with himself because he'd clinched two lucrative oil deals earlier with a couple of Chinese attendees. He had the uncanny knack of attracting money like moths to a flame. She hoped she wasn't going to be the one who got burnt.

That thought lingered as she nibbled at some mushroom polenta diamonds. She quailed and felt blood drain from her face. She leaned close to him and whispered, "Police have come in and the maître d' is pointing directly at us."

"I'm sure it's nothing to worry about." Anton quaffed the rest of his Grande Année Bollinger champagne.

Two uniformed officers wended their way through the tables. The inquisitive stares of the people at the other tables followed them. The cops kept their hats on. And stopped when they reached their table.

A slight polite bow was followed by a deep voice: "I am Inspector Bai and this is my sergeant. I am sorry to intrude, but I have reason to believe that you have committed a capital crime and I require you to join me at the dockside, where we will search your boat, the *Izolda*.

Belofsky stood up, removed his napkin and wiped his mouth. "What on earth are you talking about?"

"I have explained. Do I need to repeat myself?"

Throwing the napkin on the table, Belofsky snarled, "Don't you know who I am?"

"Yes, we know you, Mr. Belofsky. Sir, you are a foreign national who is facing very grave charges." The inspector glowered at Alita and added, "And that requirement to accompany me applies to you as well, Señorita Lopez."

The sergeant fidgeted with a set of handcuffs.

"Alright, there's no need for them," Belofsky said.

"We'll come quietly. But tell me, what do you hope to find?"

"Drugs—specifically opium."

Belofsky let out a barking laugh. "That's absurd! The Opium Wars ended long ago!"

"That is an inappropriate remark, sir," the inspector responded.

Alita got to her feet, gripped her handbag and moved to stand next to Anton. She squeezed his arm, whispered, "Don't antagonize the inspector, darling, please."

Exhibiting signs of an impending tantrum, he pushed her hand away. Now she knew where she stood —and it was no longer alongside him. She was being cast off, put adrift.

Oblivious of the body language between them, the inspector said, "The opium wars you refer to are indeed in the past, sir. Now, we are fighting a new war—against international crime."

Alita decided to try once more. "The girls, Anton," she whispered in his ear, "what about the girls?"

Her words finally sank home and he paled. He faced the inspector, hands rubbing together. "Do we really have to go now?" His tone was devoid of the earlier arrogance.

"Yes, I insist," said the inspector.

This was it, then! Instinctively, Alita withdrew her Beretta from the clutch bag and shot Anton in the chest. In the same instant, she shoved the table edge against the legs of both the inspector and his sergeant and they fell backward into a couple at another table.

People all around them shouted and screamed; a few ducked to the floor, hiding behind their tables.

Gripping her gown with one hand, she leaped onto the stage.

As she landed, she stumbled in her high heels, but kept her footing.

Anton's words rang in her ears: "Alita, why? I helped you escape!"

Taking advantage of her deadly diversion and ignoring him, she pushed aside the singer, and hurried behind the left-hand flat. She darted across the back stage and down a flight of steps. She pushed the bar on the emergency exit door and stumbled into an alley. At the end she spotted a taxi rank.

By the time she reached the front cab she was breathless and leaned in the driver's window. She remembered the name of Sara Whitney's hotel, told him, pronouncing it carefully. He frowned, so she repeated it and he nodded, said, "Get in, Miss. I take you." Lucky she'd found a cab driver who knew a little English, she supposed.

It didn't take long. The taxi driver parked opposite the hotel. "Your hotel, Miss. That will be..." She clubbed him on the head with the butt of her gun. He slumped unconscious, propped against the driving wheel; at least he didn't press against the horn.

She checked left and right and was assured that nobody was in the immediate vicinity. She put the Beretta in her bag, opened the door and slid out.

Skipping between passing cars and bicycles, she crossed the street.

Standing to the right of the hotel entrance was an elderly woman selling flowers, bunches of variegated colors on display in tall gray metal vases. Alita snatched a bunch of red peonies.

The seller said in halting English, "That is a good choice, Miss. Peony bring you prosperity. That will be…"

"Not for you it won't!" Alita gave the woman such a glare that she backed off.

Alita flounced into the hotel and strode purposefully across the foyer, the flower stalks dripping on the floor as she went.

Casting a disapproving eye at the flowers, the male receptionist said, "Can I be of assistance, Miss?"

Alita asked for the room of Mr. Brin.

"That will be 304, Miss. I'll phone to let them know they have a visitor."

"No," Alita said, offering a smile, holding up the peonies. "I want to surprise them."

"Very well, Miss."

Making her way to the elevators, Alita only harbored thoughts of shooting Sara Whitney. It had to be her; she must have escaped from the yacht somehow and alerted the police. She swore under her breath as she reached the elevator doors and pressed the "up" button. She felt conspicuous in her gown, standing here while flowers dripped on the toes of her high heels.

Finally, the elevator arrived and the doors slid open.

When she reached the third floor, she spotted the sign to rooms 301-314 and hurried that way, striding along the carpeted corridor, the Beretta now in her hand, mostly concealed by the peonies.

Stopping at room 304, she rapped on the door with the heel of the gun's grip.

A woman yelled, "Just a moment!"

Alita raised the peonies—and the Beretta—to midriff height in anticipation. She must get even, kill

Whitney and Brin. She'd been through hell because of that woman!

The door opened and Alita fired at the woman. In that split second she saw high cheekbones, black hair cut in a bob, thin lips, mouth quite wide, and dark eyes, and realized that it wasn't Sara Whitney but a stranger!

"*Daphne!*" Sara Whitney's voice.

Incensed and frustrated at having failed a second time, Alita lifted her dress and stepped over the woman named Daphne. Her eyes were tear-filled, her vision blurred as she fired at figures who darted left and right of her, one behind a sofa, another behind an upturned table. Wood shattered and splintered, glass broke, gunsmoke filled her nostrils, and the gun bucked in her hand.

Suddenly from her left a huge dark shape descended on her and slammed her to the floor.

Brin, Gene Brin! The bastard!

But she couldn't raise her gun-hand. He knelt on her wrist.

She kept pulling the trigger, regardless; deafening.

Snarling, he grabbed her hair and bashed her head on the floor, again and again, until she heard no more shots being fired and then there was nothing, no sensation at all.

Chapter 22

Manifest Destiny

Once he had dispatched the blood sample, Song returned and cut the ropes, releasing Cat from the chair. "I have the only key and you won't be able to take it from me," he said. "I don't want to fight you. Be a model prisoner and we'll have no problems."

"You have a problem already, Mr. Song. Kidnapping is a capital offence."

"You are not exactly on the side of the law, are you? I've read Mr. Dante's dossier about what you and your boyfriend have done to Ananke."

"Don't involve Rick in this."

"Very well, if you insist."

Rubbing her wrists to restore feeling, she said, "I'd like to use the bathroom, take a shower."

"Be my guest. You'll find clean towels."

She eyed her ripped sleeve, rubbed her arm where he'd inserted the needle.

"Sorry there isn't any change of clothing." He

pointed to her backpack. "The razor wire cut your clothes badly, it seems."

"As a model, I used to be at the cutting edge of fashion, but not anymore."

"I am pleased to note that you are taking this sorry business with equanimity, Catherine."

"You've done what you were required to do, Mr. Song. I suspect that you have not taken any great pleasure in it."

"You are correct in that assumption. Security is important, but there are limits, and I fear that lately Mr. Dante is sailing very close to the reef and no amount of *guanxi* will save him..."

"Guanxi?" Cat queried.

"In the business world, guanxi is used to describe a person's network of contacts, to be called upon for favors. It helps the world go round in Asia."

"That gives me something to consider while I shower." She opened the door wide and entered the utilitarian bathroom which was devoid of windows. At least there was a proper toilet, she mused, closing the door. She noticed there was no lock on the door.

She unzipped her catsuit and stepped out of it, and piled that and her underwear on the closed lid of the toilet seat.

Standing naked, she hesitated a second or two, conscious of the very strong strange man in the adjoining room. An unwelcome flash of remembrance assailed her, and she fleetingly relived her fight with Zabala in that Tangier hotel room's shower cubicle. Then she shrugged off any misgivings. If Song had meant to ravish her he'd had ample opportunity before now.

She entered the shower cubicle, slid the glass panel door shut. A plastic bottle of shower gel hung on a cord from the faucet. She poured some gel into her palm and then turned the knob. The spray of water was warm and welcome. Her forearms were seriously bruised where she had blocked Ying's and Song's blows. A large circular bruise in the area of her solar plexus reminded her of her recent defeat. She was relieved that Song had managed to eliminate most of the pain.

As she gently lathered soap on these contusions, the ache eased a little; yet it did nothing to relieve her still uncomfortably present anxiety. The last time Dante had confronted her, he'd implied that if the DNA test proved she wasn't his daughter, all bets were off and her future was liable to be very limited indeed. Martial arts training long ago informed her there was no point in worrying. Easier said than done, when your life was in jeopardy.

She didn't linger too long, and rinsed the suds.

When she shut off the spray she felt reinvigorated, despite the hovering uncertainty about her future.

Drying in front of the mirror above the wash basin, she noted the bruise on her temple was not too prominent.

She didn't know what to make of Song. He was an Ananke security chief and in Dante's pocket—or so it appeared. Yet he was totally different to Zabala. Song was no psychotic; he'd been courteous and considerate.

Time ticked by. She was very much conscious of that. She had no idea of the distances involved, but Tokyo wasn't that far—and unless the authorities were alerted, those deadly pills could be distributed within days.

She put on her underwear and then studied her catsuit. It was grimy, stained with oil and grease, and there was the onset of stale body odor. She took the intact sleeve and ripped it out, so at least the garment was balanced. Though that meant her bruises showed. She stepped into it, zipped it up. What the hell, it wasn't as if she was strutting the catwalk at fashion week! Those days seemed far gone now.

———

RICK PACED THE HOTEL ROOM, couldn't settle. His chest felt as if it was constrained by a metal band and his stomach churned, as if his insides were quivering. Despite a raging thirst, he hadn't been able to drink or even eat anything since they all got here. He kept looking at his cell-phone, which remained silent.

Earlier, Mr. Kuang had telephoned, but he had no news.

Yubi, Bing and Linghao watched him anxiously.

When Rick's phone finally rang, he answered it at once, but it was Gene.

"Any news about Cathy?" Gene asked.

"No. I'm frantic with worry! Do you want to come over here? I'm with Yubi, Bing and Linghao."

"No, I'm with Sara at the hospital, actually..."

"Sara? Hospital? What happened? Is she alright?"

"Yes, but we've had a traumatic time of it." He explained about Alita Lopez's attack, and then added, "Daphne's going to recover. I don't know about Belofsky and Alita—I hit her head pretty hard, I was *so* angry!"

"I don't know what to say, Gene. I'm glad you're both alright and hope Daphne will pull through."

"There's a police guard on Lopez and Belofsky. If they survive, they'll be charged with a string of offences that may lead to the death penalty. I can't see the Chinese agreeing to them being extradited."

CAT OPENED the bathroom door and faced Song.

He raised himself from the chair. "Feel a bit better for the shower?"

"Yes. Thanks." She gently rubbed her bare arms. "I still ache here, though."

"Sorry about that. You have quite a number of bruises."

"I received some of these from Ying."

"Considering you had just fought him, you fought well."

She offered him a smile. "Thanks, that's a compliment from a master, I think." Rubbing her upper arms, she said, "Yubi's bruises on her face. I wondered. It doesn't seem to be your style."

He shook his head, glanced at the silent TV. Then he faced her again, bowed slightly. "I take full responsibility for the actions of my men."

"If I recall correctly, Yubi said it was the man named Enlai who hit her."

"She is a brave lady. She would not betray any information about you. Enlai became enraged. I was not fast enough to stop him, so I had to chastise him after the blow." He grinned, showing those sharp teeth. "I must admit that I was pleased you gave him a headache. He deserved it!"

His demeanor tended to ease a little of her nervousness. She sat on the sofa, fingering the damaged backpack.

"I noticed the odd interesting item in there," he said.

She looked up at him, sharply.

"I needed to be sure you were not armed. I haven't removed anything—it's your property, after all."

She opened the side-pockets and removed the lockpicks. "They come in useful."

"Especially when helping a friend to escape, eh?"

He meant Yubi. "No hard feelings about that?" she queried.

"No hard feelings. You proved to be a good friend."

She offered him a smile. Her Spanish passport was intact, fortunately. She grabbed her phone, switched it on. Battery half-full, but there was no signal.

"This basement blocks the signal," he explained. He pointed to the phone on the table top. "That's my line to the outside world."

"And to Dante."

"Yes, of course. Mr. Dante wants you within easy reach."

Interesting. "Are we still in Shanghai?"

"Yes. Not far from his office, in fact."

"Your English is very good."

He bowed slightly. "I went to an international school, learned English, Spanish and French. English is the hardest, I feel."

"I agree." *Enough small talk. Time to acknowledge*

the elephant in the room. "How long do you plan to keep me here?"

"Until the results from the DNA test are released. Then Mr. Dante will decide what to do with you."

RUAN PENG, the master of the *Qing Jade* stood on the bridge wing, watching the passing traffic—shallow-draught barges, tankers, a floating crane, other container ships, and tourist boats, nothing exceeding eight knots. It was a busy river and Shanghai had recently overtaken Singapore as the busiest port. They passed half a dozen huge cranes like robot sentinels and then he glimpsed at the mouth of the river the Wusongkou lighthouse. Soon he would be beyond that. He would be glad to be at sea again.

A loudhailer drew his attention, coming from astern.

A customs launch was creating white surging bow-waves, approaching fast.

"*Qing Jade*, stop engines!" the loud-hailer demanded. "Prepare to be boarded for an urgent inspection!"

What was this all about? Doubtless he would find out soon enough. He had no option but to obey. He acknowledged the hail from the customs launch and ordered his mate to stop engines.

When the ship's engines stopped, the launch pulled alongside and Ruan arranged for a rope ladder to be lowered over the ship's side.

Gingerly crossing from the bobbing boat to the ladder, two customs officers scrambled to the main deck. A couple of other men, these dressed in white lab coats waited at the rail of the launch.

The stony-faced officers introduced themselves, showing their badges.

"This better be good," Ruan said. "I have a schedule to keep."

"If you cooperate, it should not take long." The older officer held out a hand. "Your manifest, please."

Gritting his teeth, Ruan pivoted on his boot heel. "Follow me!" He stormed across the deck and up a series of ladders to the bridge, the customs men following.

Ruan reached the bridge wing and scanned astern. The wake of his ship trailed away, the momentum of the ship carrying it forward even though the engines had ceased to turn the screws. He noticed the *Red Lantern* closing and envied the master of that vessel. He wasn't going to be bothered by jobsworth officialdom. He shrugged to dismiss these unhelpful thoughts and stepped over the bridge threshold. He crossed to a set of drawers at the back, opened the top one and removed a dossier. Without a word, he handed it to the older customs officer who now entered and was slightly breathless. Serves him right, damn the man!

The officer opened the folder, slid a finger down the columns on the sheets and then stopped. "We want to examine this container." He showed Ruan the page.

"But that's imbedded three deep!"

"Use your crane to move the containers on top of it. We require access!"

The man's peremptory tone brooked no argument. Ruan read the list, checked the weight of the containers that had to be moved, and performed a mental calculation. He was fully aware that other ships had sunk because their loads had been poorly balanced or had shifted disastrously in a storm. He fingered his mustache. "It can be done—however, the tolerances are close to critical."

"Good. While you do that, two laboratory technicians will also come aboard. They will need somewhere to perform their work."

"The canteen?" Ruan suggested.

"That would be ideal."

"How long will this take?"

"As long as necessary. We need to break the seal of the container, extract samples; and then the lab techs will test them. So it depends on how fast you can get your crane driver to give us access."

Ruan bit on a retort and reached for his microphone. He summoned the crane driver to the bridge and resigned himself to the fact that his vessel was going to be sitting idle in the river for an hour or more.

While he waited for the crane driver, he went out onto the bridge wing. And his brow creased in puzzlement. What was going on? To the stern of his vessel the *Red Lantern* was also being hailed by officials in a customs launch.

He sensed an unwelcome looseness of his bowels and his leg muscles weakened. He swallowed but couldn't get rid of the dryness in his mouth. He broke open a cigarette pack and lit one with shaking fingers. As the smoke soothed his nerves, he hoped this had nothing to do with terrorists. Sinking a couple of container ships in the river would cause untold havoc.

Chapter 23

Relatives

C at asked, "Do you know the distance from Shanghai to Tokyo?"

Song's brow wrinkled. "Is this a test?"

"No. I wondered if you could find out." She pointed to the computer.

Without a word he stood and crossed to the table, keyed in a Google search. "The distance is about 1,700 km." She was by his side now and he peered at her. "You're thinking about the shipment that left on *Qing Jade*, is that it?"

"I am. How long before the ship gets to its destination?"

He keyed in another search query. "Roughly four days."

"And the distance to Tenerife?"

Another search. "Much greater: about twenty-five days via Suez. And that presumably is the *Red Lantern* you are wondering about?"

"Yes, it is. Do you know what they're carrying?"

"Of course. The longevity pills as we call them are

on their way to Tokyo, and the lucky cat consignment is going to Tenerife. Those cats are very popular, you know. I have one in my office, by the window. Sunlight keeps the arm waving."

"I've seen them in many Chinese restaurants. But this 'special consignment' will be even more popular," she said. "The lucky cats contain raw opium which will be used to manufacture heroin in Tenerife."

"*What?* That cannot be! Are you sure?"

"Yes, I'm sure. It was Ying who organized the entire operation. My friends and I overheard him talking about it."

"Overhearing—hearsay—is not proof."

"No, it isn't. The proof is in the lucky cat container." She reeled off the identification number and as she did so looked askance at him. "You genuinely didn't know, did you?"

"No. But this makes sense now," he mused. "Mr. Heng had discovered something amiss regarding Mr. Ying, and he had heard about a 'special shipment'—no doubt the 'special consignment' you referred to."

"Do you think Dante was aware of the opium's existence?"

He shook his head. "An important man like him? No, he would not be so foolish."

"If he has sanctioned murder," Cat went on, "I don't think a little drug smuggling would disturb his conscience."

"Murder? Surely you are mistaken, Catherine."

She clenched her hands into fists, snapped, "I am *not* mistaken!" Before he could respond, she continued in a calmer manner, "His security officer, Emilio Zabala admitted that he arranged the death of my father in a car crash."

"I am sorry to hear that. It is most worrying. I took over from Señor Zabala."

"I'm happy to tell you that you're nothing like Zabala. He's currently under arrest in Spain, by the way."

"From what you say, that is comforting to hear. I am my own man, Catherine. But is it not possible that Zabala might have been lying to you?"

"No, he did it alright. And Dante was aware of it. I don't know if he ordered my father's death. Originally, I came to Shanghai to face Dante and demand he answer me."

"Instead, you have uncovered a drug smuggling organization!"

She let out a bitter laugh. "That's not the half of it, Mr. Song."

"I can assure you, once this business with Mr. Dante is concluded, I will arrange for the *Red Lantern* to be impounded by Spanish customs."

"You mean that, don't you?"

"Most sincerely. I was raised by my grandparents in Nanjing and they instilled in me the proper code of conduct and respect. In these modern times it is not easy to abide by such a code."

"Nanjing? You come from Nanjing?"

"Yes. It is a wonderful city, a beautiful city. A center of higher learning and a living museum of our history."

"So you must be aware of the massacre in 1937."

His face grew somber and he lowered his eyes. "I had relatives who survived—very many did not."

"Those Japanese conquerors were as bad as or even worse than the Nazis."

"Nazi is a label," he said. "Some Nazis were good and were served ill. Have you heard of John Rabe?"

"No, sorry."

"Rabe was one of many Westerners living in Nanjing, a Nazi working for Siemens. As the Japanese Army advanced on Nanjing, Rabe, and others created the Nanking Safety Zone to provide Chinese refugees with food and shelter."

"Where were the zones?"

"In the foreign embassies and the University. Because of his status as a member of the Nazi party, he was elected leader of the committee."

"He sounds like a German Schindler."

"There are similarities, I suppose. He argued with the military authorities and complained, pleading the cause of the hungry refugees. Figures vary, but it's believed that he saved between 200,000 and 250,000 Chinese people from Japanese atrocities."

"What happened to him?"

"He returned to Germany in 1938 and after the war he was arrested, interrogated then let go. He had to undergo a very lengthy de-Nazification process in the hope of regaining the permission to work."

"Apart from the human tragedy, the end of the war must have been an administrative and logistical nightmare," she said. "I've read about the famous rubble ladies—*trummer fraus*—who dug Berlin from its wreckage with their bare hands, brick by brick."

"Yes. Nanjing was mostly rubble, too... Well, as Rabe was unable to support his family, they suffered from malnutrition, like so many, subsisting on wild seeds, soup, and stale bread.

"I cannot recall how, but in 1948 the citizens of Nanjing learned of the Rabe family's plight and they raised money and sent their mayor to Germany; he took food for the Rabe family. Until the communist takeover my people of Nanjing sent a food package each month."

"A good Nazi, then?"

"I do not know if he followed the Nazi doctrine, I suspect not. He was a humane man, despite the Nazi label. He died in 1950. His old residence in Nanjing is now a memorial to him."

"A sobering account, Mr. Song. The people of Nanjing are praiseworthy. Yet, alas, a handful is perhaps less so—I'm thinking of the followers of 'The Long Fist'."

Song cocked his head to one side. "I have not heard of that group."

And as she told him of the mass murder planned by The Long Fist group, Song trembled where he sat and his complexion darkened. Slowly, he stood, his huge hands clenched into wrecking balls. Fleetingly, Cat feared for her life.

He moved away, strode to the bathroom and went inside, slamming the door after him. She was left alone. She crossed the room and opened her backpack. It might only take an instant to use a lock-pick to effect her escape. She grabbed her phone; still no signal. She returned to the table and sat.

While flicking through her cell-phone's menu, she dimly heard a roaring and a wailing from the bathroom. Both Bing and Yubi had told her that Chinese, normally reserved people, wailed excessively at times of bereavement, and she recalled the television images of the families waiting for news of the missing airliner, MH370.

After several long minutes, the crying ceased and Song opened the door. He appeared composed and joined her at the table. "I was not sure that you would still be here."

"We both have business to conclude with Dante, Mr. Song. I will stay for that. And in case I need your help to stop the *Qing Jade* cargo being distributed."

He sat back and eyed her studiously. "I must admit that I have come to admire you, Catherine."

"I don't suppose you could telephone Rick, my husband—my boyfriend, no need for pretense with you —assure him that I am alright?" She showed him her cell-phone, with Rick's contact number in the menu.

WHEN RICK's phone rang and showed an unknown number, he was wary about answering it. Then, his nerves getting the better of him, he pressed the button and said, "Yes, who is it?"

"It's me, darling," Cathy said. "I'm alright."

Relief flooded through him and he sat down. "Cathy, oh, my God, where are you?"

The others rushed to his side, Yubi's face filled with anxiety.

"I can't say right now," Cathy replied. "I am unharmed."

"Is Song with you?"

"Yes..."

"What's he going to do?"

"I don't know, love. Don't worry, I'll be fine." She hung up on him.

She hung up! "Fine, she says!" he exploded.

"Hey," Bing said, "at least she's alright, that's something, isn't it?"

"Yes," Yubi added and then said hesitantly, "Did I hear that Song is with her?"

Rick narrowed his eyes, gritted his teeth. "Yes, she's with him."

Yubi touched his shoulder. "At the docks, Mr. Song said he would not harm her."

Despairing, he looked into Yubi's trusting eyes. "Song has kidnapped Cathy so he can take a blood sample. Dante is obsessed with proving she's his daughter. Whatever he finds out, her life will be altered forever!"

"The DNA test can take from twelve to twenty-four hours; it is quite a process," Cat said.

"You do not seem too concerned about the result?"

"I believe deep in here," she said, beating her chest, "Dante is *not* my father!"

"I have to ask. What do you think he will do if he discovers that you are not of his blood?"

She shrugged. "I know it sounds trite, but if I could talk to him, try to end this, get him to admit his guilt, maybe then I can get a measure of closure."

"And then would you not want revenge?"

"That need for vengeance has kept me going for years, Mr. Song. You're aware of what I've accomplished. But now I have come to the conclusion that it is time that I got a life."

He offered a smile. And those sharp teeth didn't look threatening at all. "Well, let us hope it will not be too long before we hear the result."

She knew that normal DNA paternity tests usually joined a massive backlog queue. But she believed that Dante had enough clout in the right quarters to hurry along the process. Perhaps he had a tame DNA specialist in Beijing.

WHEN THE TELEPHONE rang it alarmed them both. Cat's mouth went very dry as Song answered it, switching to speaker mode. "Mr. Dante," he said in greeting. Then he asked, "Have you the DNA results, sir?"

"No, I haven't!"

Dante sounded petulant.

"Then, what can I do to help you, sir?"

"I'm phoning to learn what happened at the dockside!"

"I apprehended Catherine Vibrissae, as I told you."

"The ships—*Qing Jade* and *Red Lantern*—they were alright, the consignments were loaded?"

"Yes, sir. I saw them myself. The ships cast off at about the same time that I captured Catherine Vibrissae."

Dante swore. "Something has gone wrong. Both ships have been stopped in the river and are being searched as we speak!"

Song's gold-flecked eyes shone at Cat.

Her heartbeat raced and she almost wanted to hug him. Bing had managed to goad the authorities into action.

"That is most unfortunate, sir," Song said, calmly, "but it has nothing to do with me or my recent activities. Surely, you are not aware of anything untoward in the consignments?"

"Of course there's nothing wrong with them! It's her, I'm sure of it. Vibrissae meddling!" He paused and then snapped, "Alright, then. I will be in touch when I have the results." The line was cut abruptly.

GILDA TURATI ARRIVED at the hotel, unpacked, showered and toweled herself dry. She doused herself with expensive perfume and put on a jacquard rose shift dress and cropped red jacket, confident that it would quicken Loup's pulse when he laid eyes on her.

Sitting on the bed, she telephoned her contact. "Is the aircraft ready?"

"Yes, Ma'am," said the pilot of a private helicopter that she'd ordered. Loup was expecting a helicopter to collect him from his office roof and take him directly to the airport. She'd sworn his secretary to secrecy and now planned to arrive in that very aircraft and surprise him. The rescheduled flight to Rome would allow them to enjoy a night of passion overlooking the Shanghai skyline. She trembled with anticipation at the prospect.

"Very good," she said. "Collect me from the hotel roof in an hour."

DESPITE EXPECTING THE CALL, when the telephone rang a second time, both Cat and Song jumped. He again put the phone on speaker and answered, "Hello."

"Mr. Song?" A woman's voice.

"Yes. Is that Zou Peizhi?"

"It is, sir. I will now put Mr. Dante on the line."

The line clicked as Dante's secretary transferred the call.

Dante said, "Mr. Song, I have the results."

"That's good news, sir. But the ships, sir...?" Song said, changing the subject. "Do you know what has happened?"

"It is too early to say. There has been no communication from the authorities apart from notifying me that both vessels have been waylaid. It is annoying, as I have a flight to Rome scheduled. I don't know why this has happened. As I told you, the consignments are legitimate, after all."

"I regret to inform you, sir, I have learned that both consignments are anything but legal."

"You—you can't be serious!"

"I am, sir. My source has confirmed that drugs are being smuggled in one of our containers on the *Red Lantern*. And the *Qing Jade* container is filled with an adulterated product engineered by political terrorists!"

"This—this can't be happening to me!" Dante swore, and then added, "Who is your source?"

"Catherine Vibrissae."

Dante swore again. "The bitch! She must be responsible, then. She has planted the stuff to impugn me and Ananke!"

"No, she didn't, sir. And I know that for a fact."

There was silence at the other end and then, finally, Dante said, "Mr. Song, you have done well."

"Thank you, sir."

"Where is Catherine Vibrissae right now?"

"Sitting beside me, Mr. Dante."

"I can tell you with complete confidence that she is *not* my daughter."

Song raised an eyebrow at Cat.

Giving Song the thumbs up, she held a hand across her chest and sighed quietly.

"What happens to her now, sir?" Song asked.

"I want nothing more to do with that troublesome woman. Dispose of her. With extreme prejudice."

Chapter 24

Into Thin Air

When they'd left the basement, Song had taken Cat to her hotel, where she was met by Bing, Yubi, Linghao and a jubilant Rick.

"Your arms, you're hurt!" Rick exclaimed, holding her. Then he eyed Song. "Who's this?"

Yubi gasped. "It's Mr. Song."

"What the hell's *he* doing here?"

Cat hugged him, held him back. "Song's on our side, Rick." She'd fallen into calling him that rather than "Mr. Song" or his first name Chong, and he'd seemed happy enough about it.

"But you vanished from the dockside—and it was him who—who..."

She kissed him, and then broke free. "I haven't got time to argue now. I need a change of clothes!"

Rick stared at her, bemused.

"Talk to Song while I change," she said. "He'll bring you up to speed."

Song grinned, revealing those sharp teeth.

Rick looked alarmed.

"Don't worry, darling," Cat said, opening the bedroom door, "he doesn't bite."

Song winked at him and lowered his huge frame to the sofa.

Cat decided to wear her Temperley waterfall shirt dress as its sleeves would cover her bruised arms. It was lightweight cotton voile, with a pleated trim and a full skirt, so she'd be cool enough traipsing through the streets of Shanghai.

When she returned to the lounge, she was pleased to note that Song and Rick were chatting, and all sign of animosity had evaporated. Apparently, they'd been kept up to date with phone calls from Mr. Yuang, the port official.

"Let's go and pay Dante a visit, Song."

"What about me—us?" Rick said, standing up.

"No, this has to be between me and Dante. Song is going to help me gain access to Dante's office."

"Oh, Cathy," Rick pleaded, "I don't think this is a good idea!"

"Don't worry, I will be with her," said Song. "She will not come to harm."

Yubi gave him a dubious glare.

"I'll call you on my cell-phone," Cat said and they both left.

GILDA CLIMBED into the helicopter with a little wobble on her high heels, but steadied herself and buckled up.

The combination of the rotors and the engine proved deafening.

The pilot advised her they'd reach the hotel roof in about ten minutes, adding, "Mr. Dante's secretary has informed me that he is waiting there now. He is unaware of the alteration in his schedule."

She knew Loup didn't particularly like surprises, but she was sure that he'd relish their early reunion.

"HELLO, MR. SONG." Zou Peizhi, Dante's secretary, stood as Song and Cat entered her ante-office. The place tended to resonate with the vibration from the external air-conditioning units. The air was cool, a pleasant contrast to outside.

"We have come to see Mr. Dante," Song said.

"I am sorry. You do not have an appointment."

"It is vital that we see him now," he insisted.

"Who is this lady with you?"

"An important business associate," Song said.

"Well, I am sorry, but you are too late. Mr. Dante is waiting for his helicopter," Zou Peizhi said. "He has a flight to Rome scheduled..."

Taking Cat's hand, Song said, "I know where to go, come with me!"

Zou Peizhi took a pace round her desk. "But..."

Ignoring her, they rushed out of the door, hurried up a narrow flight of concrete stairs, and passed through a doorway leading onto the roof.

Dante stood alone, to one side of the painted white 'H' on the roof. At his side was a matching suitcase and carry-on case. He wore a cream lightweight suit with an open-necked blue shirt. He hadn't changed since she'd last seen him: the same pasty complexion and thinning gray hair, the same lopsided face; pencil-width whiskers extended from the bottom lip to the cleft chin, and he still sported a waxed mustache with curled tips. His dun-colored eyes widened at sight of her. "Mr. Song, I thought I told you to get rid of this woman?"

"I do not know what kind of man you wanted to replace Mr. Zabala, sir, but you are mistaken if you believe I would murder for you."

"Murder? Who said anything about murder?"

Cat strode forward. "Do you admit that you arranged for my father to die in that car crash? Well, do you?"

"You're still fixated on that, are you? What if I did admit it? It would be my word against yours—and Song's, presumably."

"My father had been your friend!"

"He stole your mother from me. I tried enticing her to return to me that time when she was low, but she still went back to him. I'd have given everything to win her! It pains me to look at you. When I see you, I see *her!*"

"That's no reason to have my father killed!"

"He was going to arrange a loan to block my takeover. I couldn't let him do that!"

Tears streamed down her face as she stood in front of him, her back to the parapet of the roof. She clenched her fingers into fists and used the knuckles to wipe the tears. "That's why I've sabotaged you at every chance I got—so you won't get away with his murder!"

"You stupid bitch, I didn't kill him—Zabala did."

"He followed your orders!" She pointed a finger. "You're as guilty as hell!"

Dante turned to Song. "I'm disappointed in you.

Siding with her. You're finished in Shanghai, you know. You won't get another job here."

Huge broad shoulders hunched phlegmatically. "I have decided I don't want to work for you anyway."

"You came to an arrangement, is that it? Did she seduce you, eh? The Stockholm syndrome, I imagine!"

"Don't be so—so crude!" Cat snapped.

"Crude?" Dante folded his arms across his chest and snickered, showing yellowed teeth.

Song took a step closer to Dante. "Have a care. Catherine and her friends have saved your company from ruin today."

"Catherine Vibrissae has hurt me time and again, you fool! And now you say those two ships stuck in the river are her doing? How does that save Ananke, eh?"

"The *Red Lantern* is transporting raw opium from your Wuxi factory."

"That's absurd. They're waving cats, my ex-wife's obsession. Nothing more!"

"Ying has been arrested and the evidence is plain; he's guilty."

"My God, that's...plain stupid. It was his plan? He'll face the death penalty!"

"Yes, he will."

"What about the *Qing Jade*? Ying can't be involved there."

"It's worse," Song said. "Some workers at the Nanjing factory have adulterated your goji berry pills and had intended poisoning thousands of Japanese. Chemists are testing the pills on the ship right now."

Dante spread his hands. "But I had nothing to do with that!"

"We know—and the authorities know, too. But if

the group had got away with it, in six months' time Ananke would have been ruined when the truth got out and the deaths mounted."

Dante stared at Cat, his brow creased. "You saved my company from almost certain ruin. Why?"

She trembled as she tried to contain her rage. "You need to ask?"

"Yes. Tell me."

"Letting those consignments go would have destroyed Ananke in time, but it would have been at the cost of thousands of lives. I don't want any lives on *my* conscience!"

"Oh, there you go again!" Dante snapped. "My conscience is none of your business, you stupid woman!"

Her heart hammered in anguish. This was the man she hated, and no amount of arguing would make him admit his culpability. "I came here in the hope we could end it. If you'd been reasonable and shown remorse, then—"

"Then what?" Dante laughed, dun-colored eyes twinkling. "We'd kiss and make up, eh? I think not. Besides, you're too young for me and anyway I'm about to marry for the fourth time." He glanced at his watch. "You're going to make me late. I have a flight to Rome." He peered at the skyline spread before him. A dot approached, closer by the second. "That'll be my helicopter."

Impulsively, Cat moved forward and slapped Dante across the cheek. God, that felt good! "You arrogant bastard!"

He staggered at the unexpected blow. Raising a hand to his face, he glared. "You shouldn't have done that," he said, his tone cold, rumbling from his chest.

Without warning, Dante charged at her, his arms wind-milling. She attempted a forearm block but the unexpected onrush of madness empowered him and he brushed her defensive measure aside, lunged and snarled, "You'll no longer cause me pain and anguish!"

The back of her legs hit the edge of the roof's parapet and she let out a yell as her calves slammed into the concrete. Totally unbalanced with his weight and the impetus of his attack, she toppled backward.

Instinctively, she clasped Dante's suit jacket to arrest her fall but all she managed was to pull him with her into thin air.

———

GILDA STARED out of the cockpit as the helicopter descended toward the big painted 'H' on the office building's roof. A warm feeling of anticipation welled inside her. If her marriage to Loup was destined to be brief, she intended to enjoy every second of it. Afterwards, as the grieving widow again, she'd find ways to exert the additional power that Ananke would bestow.

Her heart gave a little leap and her throat constricted briefly. There was Loup!

But he was with two other people: a woman and a big Chinese man.

They were shouting at each other.

What was going on?

Suddenly, her heart somersaulted and she gasped as Loup charged at the woman and then they both fell off the side of the roof.

Chapter 25

"You will pay..."

C at's left shoulder hit the hard metal surface of an air-conditioning unit. It creaked and its fittings groaned. Unable to find anything to grab, she slid toward the edge. As she dropped off, she snatched madly at the metal grille, fingers of both hands curling round the bars at the bottom. Her finger joints were inches from the whirring fan. The machine rattled and rumbled, as if the compressor had a problem. She had a problem, too; the grille wouldn't sustain her weight for long, the thin metal was already bending; and her fingers hurt.

This was nothing like strengthening her fingers dangling on a hangboard. Her bruised arms tensed as she hung there, swaying in space, muscle burn threatening to break her grip.

She peered over her shoulder. Dante was hanging from an adjacent unit, whimpering, holding onto the grille with one hand; his left arm was held close to his chest, a couple of fingers bloody. He hadn't been so lucky with the fan.

Beneath the unit were the support brackets, almost at her eye level. If she could reach one of them; that would transfer her weight and probably give her more purchase and ease the pain in her fingers.

"Help me!" screamed Dante. "Please!"

A helicopter hovered close by, its sound loud but not deafening. That must have been what Dante was waiting for, she realized. She glimpsed it from time to time as it moved to and fro, tantalizing but useless. There was no possibility of the pilot saving her or Dante, though, as it was obviously a commercial craft and wouldn't have rescue equipment onboard.

"CAN'T YOU SAVE HIM?" Gilda yelled at the pilot.

"No, Signora, I can't get near. The rotors would hit the building!"

"Haven't you got a winch or something?" she pleaded.

"No, ma'am, sorry. We are not outfitted for a rescue procedure. I will radio for the fire department; they should be able to get a ladder up there."

"Yes, do that!" She pressed a hand against the window. "Hang on, Loup!" she cried hoarsely, her mouth unusually dry. But there was no possibility of him hearing her.

She bit her lip, clutched her hands to her breast and watched helplessly.

"GIVE ME YOUR HAND!" Song called down to Cat.

He leaned over the parapet, his long arm reaching for her, but still too far away. Maybe this time she'd be glad of his almost simian limbs. If she pulled herself onto the unit again, she'd be able to grab his big hand.

"Leave her!" Dante screamed. "I can buy you any number of women! *Save me!*"

Ignoring him, Song shouted, "Come on, Catherine. Hurry!"

Cat decided to risk it. She kicked off her shoes. Her bare feet should give her a better grip.

Removing her right hand from the grille, she released a slight groan as her left hand now took all her weight.

The grille creaked.

She leaned to the right and felt for the support bracket.

Yes, there was a gap between the unit and the bracket; the bolts were cushioned by rubber pads, providing that gap and supplying protection for the unit. Sliding her right hand in the gap, she took a little of her weight with that hand and then released her left hand. At the same moment while hanging onto the bracket with her right hand she swung her legs toward the brick wall of the building, her dress billowing in an updraft.

Calling upon her free climbing experience, she hooked the toes of her right foot into the grout gap between two bricks. It was a narrow rough ridge, hard but firm and her toes held. That gave her the support she needed.

The muscles in her calf strained as she took her weight on the left foot, so she swiftly fastened her left hand onto the support bracket as well.

Slowly, she let out a long breath, and her chest heaved. If she'd been in better shape, not so badly bruised by Ying and Song, she'd have been able to free climb the brick building. But she couldn't rely on her wrists; they were liable to weaken without warning before she reached the top.

GILDA FLINCHED AS SHE WATCHED. The grille that Dante clung to with one hand was starting to buckle; two prongs had sprung from their sprocket holes. The look on his face was abject fear, the blood draining from him. He mouthed something, but Gilda couldn't hear him, even though she'd opened the window. The din from the helicopter was too loud.

"I should land, Signora," the pilot bellowed. "Maybe I could offer help."

"How will you help him?"

"I don't know!"

"The fire department, they are coming?"

"Yes, Ma'am. I have radioed."

"Then we must pray they will be in time." She peered at the big Chinese man leaning over the parapet. He repeatedly stared up at her. She didn't like the look of him at all.

What rankled more was her ignorance of the relationships below. Who was that woman hanging on the other unit?

Now, Cat could use the brick wall for purchase and gingerly felt the back of the unit, found a thin water hose that resisted her initial pulling action.

Hand over hand, bare toes finding gaps in the grout, she climbed until she was level with the top of the unit. It was not so easy in a dress, but she coped, avoiding her legs getting caught in the material.

Then she hooked her feet on the bracket and began to haul herself up. For a tense second or two the skirt of her shirt dress snagged on a protruding spoke from the grille and impeded progress. She tugged and the material ripped and she continued pulling herself up. Finally, she knelt on the top of the unit for a second, getting second wind.

The helicopter still hovered. Why didn't they land and offer help?

It didn't matter for at last she was within reach of Song's hands.

She jumped up, both of her hands grasping Song's. He clamped onto her wrists and it hurt, but she ignored the pain as he clung on.

With surprising ease he heaved her up.

She scrambled onto the parapet and then off it and landed on the surface of the roof.

"Thanks, Song!" She gasped, got to her feet, the rough surface scratchy on her bare soles.

"I can't reach Dante," he said.

For a fleeting second, Cat hesitated. All these years she'd wished Dante dead. Yet now, if he were to die due to her inaction, she wouldn't be able to live with that. She gestured at the suitcases. "Can you use the follow-me case? Its handle telescopes."

"It's worth a try." He loped to the cases, hooked a

hand in the follow-me handle and then returned, moving further along the parapet, directly above Dante. He telescoped the handle to its full extent, locked it and held onto the bottom of the case, its wheel bracket, and then lowered the case over the parapet. "Here, grab hold of the handle and I'll pull you up!"

"THEY'RE TRYING to pull him up!" Gilda bawled at the pilot. "Can you land now?"

"Yes, neither of them is in the way of the rotors!"

The helicopter hovered, approaching the roof from the other side.

The downdraft from the rotors blew the big Chinese man's jacket and the woman's hair and dress.

Then the aircraft landed and the pilot cut the engine.

"I'll stay here," Gilda said. "Go and see if they need any help."

Without replying, the pilot opened his door and clambered to the roof and ran in hunched fashion across the rooftop.

Gilda could hear their voices through the open window and her heart gave another lurch.

"I only have the use of one hand," Loup cried plaintively. "I will fall if I let go to grab that!"

She couldn't contain herself any longer and climbed out of the aircraft, hurried across the roof to the parapet. She stood alongside the pilot and stared down with dread.

STRENGTH HAD RETURNED to Cat's arms. She cursed herself for being a fool and sprinted to the door that accessed the rooftop, now only vaguely aware of the gritty hard surface underfoot. On one side of the doorway there were two fire-extinguishers—CO_2 and foam. On the other side was a coiled hosepipe in its glass case. Using her elbow, she broke the glass door of the hose housing and snatched the nozzle, began tugging at it. She called to Song: "We'll use this instead!" she told him.

Song pulled up the follow-me case and discarded it.

The hose didn't uncoil too easily, and she faltered in her pace twice. Then the pilot from the helicopter joined her and helped uncoil it from the casing. She made better progress then. Thankfully, it was a long hose and there was an ample length to spare to dangle over the side of the building.

Song was at her side. "What do you want to do?"

"Can you take my weight as well as his?" she asked.

"Yes." His tone implied *of course*.

Without another word, she climbed onto the coping of the parapet. An updraft of air made her skirt billow. Pushing her skirt down, she looped the end of the hose round her waist and threaded the nozzle through, making a knot that wouldn't slip and possibly cut her in half. Then she looked at Song. "Ready?"

He gripped the hose, leaving her enough slack, and said, "Yes. Go when you're ready!"

It was a while since she'd abseiled down a cliff, but this wasn't dissimilar. Holding tight, her arms taking the weight rather than her waist, she backed over the edge, her bare feet padding on the brick side of the building. She didn't have to move her hands on the hose; Song slowly eased it through his own hands, and in this manner she backed toward Dante.

"Please hurry!" pleaded the woman from the helicopter.

Cat was sweating by the time she planted her bare feet on the smooth metal surface of the top of the air-conditioning unit.

Sweat mixed with grime covered Dante's face. Below her, he stared, stark fear in his eyes, and something else she couldn't determine.

"I'll come alongside you," she said, "then help you get onto the top of the unit. Alright?"

"Yes," he croaked. "Be quick...I can't...hold on much longer."

"Song!" she called. "Lower me another two feet!"

As he did so, she edged to the side of the unit and was soon eye-level with Dante. "I'm going to grab you and then we'll haul you up."

"Don't talk about it, do it!"

No please or thank you. Slowly, so as not to jolt Song, she swung toward Dante, wrapped her legs round his waist and steadied herself. Dante grunted and wheezed through his teeth. Doubtless her weight was making his hold intolerable.

"Song, get ready for his weight!" Then she put her arms under Dante's armpits and encircled him. "Now, Dante, *let go!*"

"I can't, I can't!"

"Hurry, damn you! Song can't hold us both for long!"

"I'll fall—you'll cast me down, I know you will!"

Infuriated with the man, she shouted, "Song, pull

us up!" She counted on Dante having little strength left to resist.

Dante screamed as his hand was yanked from the grille; he clutched it to his chest and whimpered. "My hands!" He trembled as they were slowly hauled higher, past the conditioning unit.

"Keep still," Cat told him, "you're not making it easier!"

Dante half-turned in her arms, glared at her. "I'll make you pay for what you've done to me!"

Unexpectedly, he wrapped an arm round the hose, above her hands. His eyes flared wildly as he used his injured free hand as a fist and struck her jaw. He screamed as he hit.

Sharp pain lanced through her lips. They both jerked on the hose. She gasped, tried to heave in air as the hose around her waist dug into her; maybe the knot hadn't been tied properly, maybe it was the nozzle that was digging in: whatever the reason, she was finding it difficult to breathe.

The fool didn't seem to comprehend that she was tied to the hose.

He hit her again and cried out in self-inflicted pain.

They both swung hard against the brick wall and her head struck it with considerable force.

Before blackness overtook her she had the vague impression of Dante spiraling away from her, yelling; then only blackness.

She couldn't have been unconscious for long, maybe mere seconds. Her senses returned as she was heaved onto the parapet and then lowered to the safety of the roof surface.

Groggy, lying on the roof, she held her head, which

throbbed unremittingly. She passed a hand over her mouth and winced; her lower lip was bleeding. Then she peered up at Song. "What happened?"

"We lost him." He dropped the hose and massaged his shoulders.

A woman's voice intruded, high-pitched, accusing. "You deliberately let him fall to his death!"

She was attractive, tanned, Latin, in her mid-forties. Her mouth was twisted in an ugly way, her big dark eyes tear-filled. She had an odd birthmark on her left temple and her long black hair flew behind in a light breeze.

The pilot rushed forward, said, "Signora Turati, they tried to save your fiancé!"

The Turati woman shook her head vigorously. "No, they didn't—or he'd be here now!" She sobbed, her frame shaking violently.

Song gave Cat a hand, helped her up. Once she was on her feet, she felt unsteady, woozy. He stepped close to support her.

"We tried... He fought me," Cat said, lifting a hand to her temple. That too came away with a little blood. The throbbing persisted. She could do with Song's magic pain-relief manipulation.

"I don't know who you are," the Turati woman snarled, "but you will pay for what you've done today!"

My God, she sounds like Dante.

Trembling, staring, the woman seemed deranged.

"Signora Turati, please," urged the pilot, gently taking her arm.

The woman gave Cat and Song a final stare that contained naked malice, pivoted on her heel and strode back to the helicopter. "You will rue the day you let Loup Dante die!"

The fire department siren sounded, getting close, but then it was drowned by the engine and rotors of the aircraft.

The helicopter lifted into the sky and veered away.

Cat saw the woman peering at her, and a chill ran along her spine.

Epilogue

Vile Shade

The private room of the Japanese embassy was filled with Chinese and Japanese officials and members of the press. Cameras flashed. Standing in front of the podium were Bing, Linghao, Yubi, Song, Rick and Cat. She wore a Stella McCartney leopard print silk dress, with fitted waist and gently flared skirt and a fairly modest V neckline. She'd applied make-up to conceal her various bruises. Song and Rick appeared smart in their tailored lightweight beige suits. The others had decided to attend in modest Chinese attire.

The Japanese ambassador stepped onto the podium, solemn in his pin-stripe suit and tie. He adjusted his spectacles and then said in measured English, "Our country is very grateful to all of you for your intervention in the notorious 'Operation Cataclysm'. We respectfully hope you will visit us one day soon."

The Chinese representative wore a business suit as well. He moved to the ambassador's side and also spoke in English: "I must add thanks from my country too. Your actions helped avert a terrible crime that could have resulted in a political cataclysm." He squinted at the Japanese ambassador. "Sino-Japanese relations are awkward at present, but this misguided act of vengeance could have been a tipping point." He clapped his hands and gestured to their left.

Two slim ladies entered. They wore traditional blue satin dresses with white and red embroidery, complemented with high tight-fitting collars fastened with toggle clasps, and short sleeves. They were very elegant, with high cheek-bones and black hair tied into buns at the nape of the neck. They carried cushions with several small gold boxes resting on them.

The ambassador presented medals to each of them, while, for the benefit of the press, the Chinese official stated, "The firm of Ananke is exonerated in this affair. Those responsible belonged to the illegal organization 'The Long Fist' and as we gather here today many of their members are being arrested and will soon face justice."

Later, as they all circulated with cocktails and answered questions from journalists, Cat wondered about Dante's fiancée, Gilda Turati. In the interim before this official presentation, she'd asked Song to investigate and he'd provided her with considerable information about the Turati business empire. If Gilda Turati hadn't already discovered Cat's identity, the news reports would reveal more than enough to satisfy her curiosity.

Although Loup Dante was dead, Cat experienced no release. Quite the opposite. It was fanciful, she knew, but it was as if his vile shade hovered over her;

she sensed his astral presence and feared she'd never shake it off.

She needed to concentrate on a new life, where there was no place for a vendetta against Ananke. Let the vengeance die with Dante. This was the end of her crusade. A new life. Now, that was a wonderful thought.

"Penny for your thoughts," Rick whispered. He clasped her hand, his touch sending a tingling jolt through her.

"Actually," she said, "I was thinking I'll soon be thirty and my body-clock is ticking."

"Clocks do that, you know." He brushed his brown hair with his free hand. "Time waits for no man—or woman. I'm getting gray streaks."

"I was going to say gray suits you. But if you're concerned you probably just need to re-dye it. Actually, I liked the original black, too. If we were to get married, you might end up with more gray hairs—would you like to have children?"

His gray-blue eyes sparkled. "In the plural?"

She shrugged and laughed. "Who knows? One to begin with, perhaps."

"Yes, I'd love to have a child...or two... Is this a marriage proposal, Mrs. Moreno?"

She flushed pleasurably, a fluttering in her stomach. "I think it is. Let's finally make it legal, Mr. Barnes," she purred, leading him through the French doors, onto the patio and deep into the embassy's exotic Chinese garden.

Acknowledgments

My thanks to Gordon Faulkner for checking my insights into China. Gordon is the author of *Managing Stress with Qigong*. Any errors remaining are mine alone!

A Look At: Rogue Prey

A Leon Cazador Thriller

Each hunter has the same equipment—a sniper rifle, five bullets and a machete. An even killing field.

A corrupt organization in Spain is selling the ultimate thrill. They cater to rich amateur game-hunters who hunger for the privilege of stalking and killing human prey. Their targets are non-persons. In effect, the vile process gets rid of illegal immigrants.

Enter Leon Cazador—a half-English, half-Spanish private investigator who occasionally assists the authorities. Eager to take down this immoral organization, he's tasked with going full cloak-and-dagger.

But when his cover is blown and he's forced to join nine other captives, will he become the hunters' ultimate prey?

AVAILABLE NOW

About the Author

Nik Morton has sold over 100 short stories, edited periodicals and contributed to magazine articles, chaired writers' circles, run writing workshops, and judged competitions. He has edited many books and was sub-editor of the monthly magazine *Portsmouth Post* (2003-2007) and Editor in Chief of a U.S. Publisher (2011-2013). He has had 32 books published —including 3 books in the psychic spy *Tana Standish* series and 8 westerns—and co-written 4 books in the *Floreskand* fantasy series. His *Write a Western in 30 Days – with plenty of bullet points!* is a best-seller. With his wife Jennifer, Nik lived in Spain for several years (2003-2019). They have since returned to England, residing in Northumberland—near their daughter Hannah, son-in-law Harry and grandchildren Darius and Suri.